BOOTS AND SADDLES

MG XX K.H

PY

BOOTS AND SADDLES

Chet Cunningham

A Lythway Book

CHIVERS PRESS
BATH

First published 1988
by
Dorchester Publishing Co Inc
This Large Print edition published by
Chivers Press
by arrangement with
Dorchester Publishing Co Inc.
1990

ISBN 0 7451 1224 2

Copyright © 1988 by
Chet Cunningham/BookCrafters
All rights reserved

British Library Cataloguing in Publication Data

Cunningham, Chet *1928-*
  Boots and saddles.
  I. Title
813.54 [F]

ISBN 0-7451-1224-2

I

FORT WALLACE, KANSAS. August, 1868:

Lieutenant Paul Winfield never saw the fist coming. It slammed into the side of his face as he stood yelling at several masked figures who had stormed into his bachelor officer's quarters at Fort Wallace.

The heavy blow smashed Winfield to the side and he dropped to his knees, shaking his head trying to clear it. He flailed his arms to keep from falling on his face. Quickly, his senses cleared and bitterness flooded his face as he jumped up. He was forced back against the two-by-fours of the single wall construction of the army fort at the far western border of Kansas.

Five masked officers of the United States Army stood in front of him. All had jackets on to hide their military rank. Not one of them had spoken since they stormed into his quarters slightly after midnight.

Winfield stood in his long johns ten feet

from his bedroom and without a chance to get to a weapon.

"I'll have your asses for this!" Winfield bellowed.

One of the officers drew a saber from behind him and swung it up until it was positioned an inch from Winfield's throat.

"Now hold on! So far this has been only slightly illegal. Now you're moving toward some serious criminal prosecution here in a real court martial."

One of the men laughed. Winfield looked at the man. He knew the laugh, knew the man, but he wouldn't let on, not now.

"I don't know who any of you are, but I'll find out, and when I do, you'll all pay one way or another."

A saber slashed forward, stopped an inch from Winfield, then sliced through his long johns sleeve and stabbed into the pine siding of the outer wall.

Winfield gave a startled cry as the saber drew a blood line across his shoulder as it scraped past. No sooner was that one in than another long knife jabbed into the wall, cutting through his long john underwear, but this time near his crotch.

Someone else laughed.

The saber point at his throat never wavered. All of the man's face Winfield could see were the malevolent brown eyes, slightly crinkled at the corners. Winfield hadn't been here at Fort Wallace long, so he couldn't identify the man by his eyes. But he would in the future. He would find these bastards!

Two more sabers sliced past flesh through his underwear pinning him to the wall. The heavy weapon at his throat lifted and delicately cut a thin line of blood across his forehead. Winfield screeched more in surprise than pain. Then the four sabers pinning him to the wall came out slowly, drawing blood on both his shoulders and thighs. He screamed in sudden pain. Then the long knife that had been at his throat came forward again and slashed across his cheek deep enough to leave a scar.

A falsetto voice daggered into the silent room.

"You have been here only a short time, Winfield, but you have earned our wrath. You will never be happy or safe here. The Brotherhood will make sure of that. You will withdraw at once your efforts to volunteer for duty with the Tenth Cavalry. They are unworthy!"

The men had been slipping out of the front door one at a time without Winfield noticing it. Now he saw that there was only him and the falsetto speaker, the one with brown eyes. As soon as the officer withdrew his sword, Winfield surged away from the wall with a roar of hatred.

He caught the man by surprise, slammed into his side, smashing the long weapon from his hand, jolting him halfway across the room before they hit the kitchen table and went down in a flailing confusion of arms and legs.

Winfield scrambled up first, kicked the other man in the side, then crashed six hard blows into the man's face and head. He sagged. Winfield hit him with a thundering right fist in the jaw, spun him around and dumped him half unconscious on the floor. Winfield heard a voice outside. He jumped to his door quickly and threw the bolt so the others could not come back. Then he hoisted the officer to his kitchen chair, tied him to it with his hands behind the back, and ripped off the bandana mask.

"Laughton!" the second lieutenant said in surprise. "Captain Harry Laughton?"

The man tied to the chair mumbled something, then regained consciousness.

"Bastard!" Laughton brayed. "Why didn't you leave it alone? Now there's no way you can go on living on this post." Laughton's eyes were angry. "Why couldn't you have left it be?"

"You assault me, you wound me, you belittle me, you insult me, and then you want to run off like the kind of cowards you five were behind your masks? What are you, Laughton, some kind of sadistic shit head? You just bought yourself enough trouble to end your military career."

Winfield untied one of the officer's hands, his right one, then so fast that Laughton could do nothing to prevent it, Winfield broke the Captain's arm across his raised knee.

For a moment the sound of the cracking arm bones hung heavy in the officer's quarters.

Then Laughton screamed.

Winfield slapped him hard, once on each side of his face. The blow was so heavy that it almost upset the chair. Laughton's scream wailed to silence.

"The names of the other three with you. I know one. Give me the other names besides Lieutantant Tryon."

The fury, the total anger in Laughton's face faded. For just a moment there was a flash of fear, then he laughed. "What good will it do you, you'll be dead within twenty-four hours."

"Not a chance. I'll never be without my weapon, and my hideout derringer, you can tell them that." Winfield slapped the captain's broken arm.

The captain in the chair bleated with pain. "Bastard!"

"I've got all night, Laughton. You've got no authority over me now. You were captured while threatening a United States Army officer. If you're still conscious by morning, you'll get to walk over to Doctor Judson's small office. The other names, now!"

After waiting a minute with no response from the man in the chair, Winfield slapped the broken arm again.

A high keening of pain seeped from Laughton's lips. Then slowly, he spoke the other three names: "Lieutenant Bartlett, Lieutenant Zennican, and Captain Oberholtzer."

Winfield straightened. "Yes, it figures. All low born, all so common and unlettered it's an amazement to me that any of you ever received commissions."

"Untie me, now," Laughton demanded.

Winfield laughed. "Yes, yes of course,

and let you go directly to the other four so you all can come back here and murder me in my bed? I expected more of you, Laughton, even with your sloping forehead and your disgusting personal habits. But I didn't think you would be quite that stupid."

Winfield moved toward his bedroom. "No, Captain, you will sit in the chair the rest of the night. In the morning I'll take you to Doctor Judson to have your arm set and splinted, then I'll march you directly to Colonel Roberts's office and charge you with assault and battery, with conduct unbecoming an officer, with torture, and as many other violations of regulations as I can produce."

"Won't work, Winfield," Laughton said through a grimace of pain. "I'll have four sworn witnesses to contradict every word you spit out. You don't have a chance. If you want to live more than 24 hours, get me over to Captain Judson's quarters within the next five minutes."

Winfield reached in his bedroom and came out with his service revolver. He pushed the polished blue steel of the issue .45 caliber six-gun against Captain Laughton's forehead and thumbed back the hammer.

7

"Do I look that brain damaged to you, Laughton. You're damned lucky I haven't pulled the trigger before now. One more word out of that ugly mouth of yours and you'll never see morning. You hear me? Don't say a word, don't even nod. Just shut your eyes and be quiet."

Captain Laughton shut his eyes.

Lieutenant Winfield watched the captain a moment, snorted and went into his bedroom. He washed off the cuts and scratches and the slice on his cheek. There was little he could do for them until morning. Perhaps Doctor Judson could bandage them.

He crawled under the covers of his bed. But he didn't sleep.

Damn, what the hell was he going to do in the morning? The four outside knew that Laughton never came out. They must suspect that he had been overpowered. They could be setting up all sorts of traps for him, all sorts of plots against him.

He had to get to the Colonel as soon as he could.

Right now!

He slid out of bed and reached for his pants, then his shirt and his boots.

Right now! He had to see the colonel!

The other four members of the Brotherhood would be waiting for him, but he would have his pistol in Captain Laughton's mouth. It would be dangerous, but he could do it!

Colonel Colt Harding woke up his first morning in Ft. Walker with a sour taste in his mouth. It was from the rotten whiskey at the welcoming party last night given for him by three majors and a captain and Colonel Roberts, commander of Ft. Wallace.

Harding had been tired after the three day horse ride from the wrecked train, and had wanted more than anything to drop into his bed. But courtesies had to be put up with. Especially since he was here on a special mission for General Phil Sheridan.

Colt kicked out of the sheet and sat up. It was hot already this morning. Good old Kansas. He had hopes of doing his job here quickly and getting back to Ft. Riley or maybe even Ft. Leavenworth where his wife Doris and the two kids were living.

Why had he been given this job? He wasn't an Inspector General. General Phil Sheridan said that Ft. Wallace was the worst unit in his command. He wanted it cleaned up, quickly, and the rotten apples thrown out of the service, no matter who they were.

Colt's orders said he would proceed to Ft.

Wallace and start up a Lightning Troop for quick strikes. That was his official job and what his orders said. He washed his face in the cold water of the bowl and dressed. His Lieutenant Colonel rank was still temporary, but it did give him more clout with the field soldiers, especially those like full Colonel Darrell Roberts.

This mess at the fort had to be laid at his feet. But how do you try to clean up something like this without telling the Fort Commander? Colt's written briefing had talked of officers beating men, of lack of discipline, of some kind of a secret society among officers, and of course all of the problems with a mixed post, where the Tenth Cavalry was quartered.

The Tenth was an all Negro regiment, black troopers with all white officers commanding them. That alone was enough for built in problems. However, the trouble did not come from the Negro troops. The Buffalo Soldiers, as the Negro troopers were called by the Indians, were some of the best Indian fighters in the army. Some said the Indians had named them Buffalo Soldiers partly because the Indians had great respect for the buffalo, and they also respected the fighting ability of the black troopers. Another theory was that the shaggy Negro troopers resembled to a degree the shaggy summer front shoulder coat of the buffalo.

In any event the Negro troopers would be part of the problem in cleaning up the fort.

Colt gave up worrying about it and headed for the bachelor officers' mess where a special cook provided meals for most of the unmarried officers. The food wasn't bad, and it was a lot better than the troopers had at either their troop or the company sized cooking facilities.

A chatter of conversation slowed and then stopped as Colt came in the mess. Gradually the fifteen officers resumed talking after he was served. He sat at a small table near a captain. He looked up at the foot soldier.

"Captain, what am I missing? It seems like there's something here I don't know about."

"Colonel, I'm sure you'll find out soon anyway. There was an accident last night. One of our officers was killed."

"Christ! The hostiles kill enough of us. What happened?"

"Nobody seems quite sure. Looks like he was trampled to death in the paddock. Nobody saw him go in there. Nobody has any idea why he would be out there after midnight. The paddock guard found him about two this morning under the hooves."

"Was he a cavalry officer?"

"No sir, that's what makes it stranger than ever. He was an Infantry Second Lieutenant."

Colt ate his breakfast quickly and went directly to the commandant's office.

"Hell of a note!" Col. Roberts thundered as soon as he saw Colt Harding walk in and close the door. "Dammit! I don't have enough problems around this bastardized fort, now I got a damned suspicious death of an officer!"

"An accident, sir?" Colt asked.

"How the hell can I tell? Looks like it. His body is over at the fort surgeon. But why would he be out there, and after midnight? I . . ." Colonel Roberts looked up. "Colonel, could I ask you to take a critical look at this case. Doesn't make sense that a man like Lieutenant Paul Winfield would let himself be trampled by horses without a shout or call. The paddock guard post is less than thirty feet from where his body was found."

Colt stood and reached for his hat. "Yes, sir, Colonel Roberts. I'd like to take a look at the situation. I'll say nothing to anyone until I report back to you."

He started for the door.

"Oh, Colonel Roberts. Would you say that things have been a little unsettled here? I mean, with the Negro troops and all?"

"Highly unsettled. We have fights between the coloreds and the whites. Every mixed post has that. But we've been having some kind of problem with the officers. Can't imagine what is going on. My own son is a First Lieutenant in an Infantry company here, but I can't get shit out of him."

Colt nodded to his superior, and walked out the door. Just how would a body look that had been trampled to death by a herd of army mounts? he wondered.

II

DOCTOR JAY JUDSON, Captain United States Army, was unlike any army surgeon Colt had ever seen. He was lean and fit, nearly six feet tall with a face almost as weathered as a trooper's. He had his hair trimmed short like the old German soldiers, and his eyes were clear and slightly angry now as he stared at Colt, then down at the naked body of Paul Winfield laying on the crude operating table in a room lighted with four kerosene lamps even during the day. They were just behind the medic's office.

"How in hell did something like this happen!" Captain Judson roared moments after they had shaken hands.

"Look at this. Both his arms are broken. Clean breaks with the bones jutting through the flesh. There are no hoof prints, no horseshoe marks on the skin."

He pointed to a gash down the side of Winfield's face. "This is a saber slash. I've patched up enough of them to know. I'd say damn few of those army mounts in the paddock were using sabers last night."

Colt smiled at the young surgeon's anger. He was starting to feel some of the same fire. "Yes, Doctor, I understood. What was the cause of death, can you say?"

"Not for sure. The body was trampled some by the horses, but none of the wounds were serious, and none of them bled. Now you know that a horse will do all it can to prevent stepping on anything, including a body. Those horses were packed together and driven over this body. But Winfield was already dead by that time."

"How can you tell, Doctor?"

"Once the heart stops pumping blood, a cut or a gash doesn't bleed. There's no inside blood pressure from the pounding, pumping heart. Now a cut might bleed a little just from gravity, like all the blood left in a body drains to the lowest point along a line of blood vessels before the blood hardens."

"So your report will say that Lieutenant Winfield was murdered, and not killed in an accident?"

"Yes, sir. Three wounds could have killed him." Judson turned the head so Colt could see the top of it. "I've shaved his head around this spot. See this deep blue wound. My guess is it was made with the butt of a .45 pistol.

He showed a small wound over the heart.

"I haven't seen a wound like this since I left Chicago's toughest streets. Looks insignificant, that wound was made by an extremely sharp knife blade no more than a quarter of an inch wide and eight to ten inches long. We used to call it a Chicago ice pick. This wound would have caused the death if the victim was still alive when it was given."

"I get the idea, Captain. Somebody

wanted this man dead, killed him after torturing him, and then tried to cover it up."

"Exactly. The third wound is the most interesting. His testicles were crushed and his penis cut almost off. Intense bleeding here could have caused death if it wasn't stopped."

"What about those slices and scratches on his shoulders and thighs?"

"They puzzle me. All of them bled, so they were made while Winfield was still alive. They are not really deep enough to indicate any serious torturing."

"Doctor, do you know anything about this young man? His service here, reputation, anything?"

"He's only been at the fort for a few weeks, three months maybe. Seemed to get along well. I heard that he had volunteered to be an officer with the Tenth. You know that's considered on this and most posts as the worst job an officer can draw."

"I've heard that. Colonel Roberts asked me to look into this matter. If anyone else inquires about the remains, I'd be pleased if you would report the names to me."

"That I can do, Colonel. I'm about as anxious as you are to see who did this. I want to look that man in the face, and then maybe punch him a couple of times."

Colt thanked the doctor and stepped outside the shiplap sided frame building. He looked around and saw two men watching him. Both turned away at once and became overly busy working on the porch of one of the frame buildings. Colt wondered if he was starting to see trouble where none existed.

He walked back to the commander's office. Wallace was a typical frontier fort. It was not a barricaded, enclosed, attack proof compound. Instead it was a motley collection of frame buildings assembled somewhat around a square parade grounds.

Since Indians seldom attacked an established army camp or facility, there was no need for fences or barricades here. This was not a hardship post so there were officer wives and children present, a big sutler's store, and stables where some of the mounts could be kept out of the weather.

As he walked along, Colt thought about the death, the savage torture murder. Colt was a tall man. At six-feet-one he stood higher than most of the troopers or officers. The average height of the men was about five-feet-six.

Colt had short cropped brown hair and brown eyes under heavy brows. He now cultivated a thick, full and brown moustache.

He had been in the mllitary service all his life. Just out of higher school in New York state, he had won an appointment to West Point. He graduated in time to see plenty of action in the Civil War where he was a company commander and rose to a brevet bird colonel rank before the court house signing ended the great war.

Because of the West Point background and record, he was reduced only to his permanent rank of Captain after the war when the army shrunk dramatically from 2,200,000 men to about 25,000 troops. He had developed the concept of a quick strike force of 50 men and called it the Lightning Troop.

He had used his Lightning Troop with good results against the Comanche in Texas and again in Ft. Phil Kearny in Wyoming. General Phil Sheridan heard of his work, agreed with the principle and came for a demonstration. Phil Sheridan soon had Colt Harding promoted and attached to his personal staff with a wide range of duties.

But he had never been called on to clean

up a fort before, let alone run into the murder of an officer.

He talked with Colonel Roberts for only a moment, confirming the suspicion that the surgeon agreed it was not an accidental death. Then he talked to the adjutant, Major Franke. The major was small, with a pot belly and spectacles. He peered over them now at Colt.

"Winfield? Yes, he was assigned as second in command with C-Company. We try to put two officers with our 50 man infantry companies. I'm going to have to see if we have a man to fill that slot."

"Any problems with him? Did Winfield have any enemies?"

Major Franke looked up sharply, his face showing a frown. "You telling me that his death was not an accident?"

"I didn't say that, Major. I'm simply trying to get some background on the man. How did he do his job?"

"No complaints from his Company Commander. You might check with him. I gave him permission to go over to Winfield's quarters and clean it out and send his personal effects—"

"Where are his quarters?" Colt asked, cutting him off.

"Oh, Officer Country number 0-16."

Colt marched out the door to the barren dust of the street in front of the adjutant's office and walked toward the officers' quarters. He found number sixteen and pushed open the door.

Three men in the room looked up suddenly.

"What the hell?" one said.

Then Colt stepped inside and they saw his shoulder rank and came to attention.

The older of the three with Captain's insignia on his shoulders turned. His right arm was in a sling on his chest and seemed to have a cast on it. He saluted left handed.

"Yes, Colonel Harding. We're cleaning up here, packing Winfield's belongings to be sent to his widow. She's back at Hays, I believe."

"I missed your name, Captain," Colt said.

"Oh, excuse me. We met yesterday. Laughton, Captain Victor Laughton."

"You didn't have a broken arm yesterday. How did it happen?"

"Too embarrassing to talk about, sir. I stumbled and fell in my quarters. Stupid of me, but there you have it."

"Sometimes those things happen. Captain, I'd like you and your men to regroup outside. Colonel Roberts has asked me to check over the quarters here. If you wouldn't mind."

"Oh, no. Course not. Fact is, you can pack and ship his gear if you want to."

Colt waved them outside and closed the door. He examined the frame and lock there carefully. There was no sign the bolt had been kicked off. These doors were no better than most on army quarters. A determined man can kick his way through most of the doors.

The two windows were also intact. Neither could be opened.

He swung the door wide to allow in more light, then lit a lamp and examined the floor. The wooden floor of these rooms were like most, one by tens butted together and nailed over joists. Some barracks and quarters floors were finished, some not. This one had not been varnished or lacquered.

Near the outer wall, Colt found several spots that had dried dark brown. He wet his finger and rubbed the spots and they turned red. Blood.

That could account for the minor wounds on Lieutenant Winfield. He could have been wounded here, captured and taken somewhere else and killed.

Major Harding found what he wanted behind some cooking staples in the small room off the living room that served some married officers as a kitchen. The book was leather bound, about five by seven inches, and had lined, blank pages. It was nearly half filled with writing. A diary. Colt slipped it into a large brown envelope he found on a shelf.

There were a dozen or more books: philosophy, English poets, American literature, economics, "The Civil War: a Study" and others. The man seemed to be well read, Colt decided.

Colt found nothing else suspicious. The officer's gunbelt hung on the back of a chair. Colt sniffed the muzzle. It had not been fired recently. If only walls could talk. He took the diary out of the envelope and pushed it inside his shirt and buttoned it, then went outside.

"It's all yours, Captain. Winfield must have been quite a reader. Did you see all those books?"

"Yes, he did read a lot," Laughton said. The three officers were leaning against the wall. "He was second officer in my Baker Troop. Did a good job."

"Carry on," Colt said and was surprised

when the three officers saluted him. He returned the salute and went out to the stables. The paddock here was a six strand barbed wire fence around an acre plot of ground next to the stables building.

Men worked there cleaning stalls, putting down fresh straw, and at one end a farrier pounded nails into a new burden shoe on a mount's hind hoof.

One of the men pointed to the spot where Lieutenant Winfield had been found.

"Where is the interior guard duty post near here?" Colt asked the trooper. The man almost froze. He had seen a light colonel in his day, but never actually talked with one before. He thawed just enough to show Colt the spot where the guard usually stood so he could see into the stable building and most of the paddock.

The place where the body had been found was within plain sight of the usual guard post.

At the guard house, Colonel Harding had the duty sergeant show him which man was on guard duty at the paddock last night. "Two men during the period of time from ten P.M. to two A.M., sir. The body was discovered shortly before two when the horses got upset in that side of the paddock."

"I want their names, Sergeant. Then send two runners to bring those men back here at once."

"Yes, sir!"

Five minutes later the two soldiers stood at attention in front of Colt who sat on the Sergeant of the Guard's desk.

"Men, in any situation like this the Army asks a lot of questions. That's what I'm doing here today. Nothing official, just a casual inquiry into the death of Lieutenant Winfield. We want to know how and why it happened."

The two fidgeted in place. The older one, probably thirty, had faded spots on his sleeves that spoke of losing stripes. The younger man was so frightened he could hardly stand up.

"Steve Sapp?" Colt asked.

"Yo. Here, sir." It was the older man.

"I understand, Private Sapp, that you were at the paddock guard post from ten P.M. to about twelve last night. Is that right?"

"Yes, sir."

"Did you hear or see anything out of the ordinary?"

"No sir, all was quiet. I did not make a call to the Corporal of the Guard."

"Private Morgan, did you hear anything until slightly before you called the corporal?"

"No, sir. It was quiet from midnight to almost near to when I called. Horses was talking and prancin' and stomping around. Just wasn't normal, sir. I been paddock guard before, sir."

Colt looked at them both with a steady, level gaze that would allow no foolishness. "Is the information you've given me the truth, the whole truth, and nothing but the truth?"

"Yes, sir!" Private Morgan said at once.

"Yo, sure as hell is, sir," Steve Sapp said.

Colt dismissed them and sat there wondering. Private Sapp was laughing at him. They both knew he was lying, but there was no way Colt could prove it, and Sapp knew it.

Colonel Colt Harding rubbed one rough hand over his face and headed back to his quarters. The diary under his shirt was starting to interest him more and more. So far somebody on this post was getting away with murder, and Colt was not going to permit that. The key might be in the dead man's diary.

III

COLT KICKED HIS feet up on the edge of the table and leaned back in the kitchen chair as he looked at the last entry in the diary of Lieutenant Paul Winfield. It was dated the day before, the same evening that he died.

I don't like it, but there's nothing I can do. I'll keep on with my job the best I can. Eventually, someone will bring them to justice.

Mistreating the enlisted men now and then is no crime in most officers' books, but what this group does is beyond belief. I saw one officer use a horse whip on one of his men. The flogging put the private on the medical report for almost two weeks. If the man complained, no one heard about it.

These officers amaze me. In civilian life I probably would never even meet or talk to those low types. Officers and Gentlemen! Ha! Nine out of ten use their officer rank as an excuse to act like they are princes of the realm and due all honors and courtesies. Ha! But someone has to bring a little class and breeding to the Army Officer Corps. It might as well start with me!

The day before Lieutenant Winfield evidently had been particularly incensed, but as Colt read the page for the third time he was still not entirely sure what the problem was.

One captain in that infamous group has me confused. When we're alone he treats me correctly, even warmly, as if he would like to absorb some polish and class. Then when his group arrives he becomes a little Caesar, demanding, obtuse, unthinking and often violent. It's as if someone pushes a nerve ending and he takes on a new personality. The man needs medical help.

Yesterday I saw two officers of the group break a corporal's arm. They had taken him behind the stables. I was in the area by chance and one of the officers ran to me and hustled me away. He made veiled threats about my personal safety if I said anything about what I had seen. I assured him I wouldn't, but in my heart I knew that I would record the incident and retain the information for my eventual talk with Colonel Roberts.

A week prior to his death, Lieutenant Winfield wrote with more candor.

I absolutely can't put up any longer with

these outrageous actions by the group of my fellow officers. They call themselves the Brotherhood, and they asked me to join them, but I politely indicated I had no wish to become one of them. They warned me not to mention the offer, or even breathe the name of their group.

I told them I had much better things to do, such as read and perhaps write some poetry or an article for a military journal. They ridiculed me and I left at once.

Colt grabbed at the name, the Brotherhood. He had heard it before. At least he had a name for them. On the same page, Colt found another shred of information that interested him.

I have decided without any chance of reversal, that I will volunteer to replace the white officer, Lieutenant Wilson, in the Tenth Cavalry. A spot is open in Charlie Troop and I'll fill it. I know that most officers consider an assignment to the Buffalo Troopers the worst in today's army. However, I will look forward to working with these men who are coming out of slavery into a free world with their dignity intact. It should remain that way, and especially in the Army of the United States of America.

I know the Brotherhood will be angry that a white officer volunteers for this duty. Whatever the group decides to do, I will counter with equal or greater force. A gentleman must defend his honor and his person with all necessary action. As I remember, Wilson died last month in a fall from his horse. When I first heard of the accident, it seemed strange. The man was a good horseman, well liked by his troops. I still wonder if the Brotherhood had anything to do with the death.

Colt closed the diary, secreted it in a spot none would think to look, and went to the Commander's office to have a talk with Colonel Roberts.

"I have heard that Lieutenant Winfield had decided to volunteer for the spot as Troop Commander in the Tenth's Charlie Troop. Is that right, Colonel?"

"We did talk about it once two weeks ago, shortly after Wilson's accident." Roberts looked up sharply. "You saying that his wanting to volunteer for duty with the Negro troops might have been a factor in his murder?"

"It's a possibility. How did Lieutenant Wilson die?"

"Freak accident. Playing a kind of polo game with mallets and a big ball. Some officers made a polo field out behind the stables. I encourage the cavalry officers to play. Figure it makes them better horsemen.

"Anyway, four riders went down in a tumble late one afternoon, almost at dark. Near as we can figure, Wilson got kicked in the head. Died on the spot. He was a good officer."

"But he was leading a black troop."

"He didn't volunteer. I had to talk with him for two hours to make him take the assignment."

"Interesting. Have there been any other accidents to white officers leading Negro troops?"

"No." Colonel Roberts looked at Colt. "You suggesting that Wilson's death wasn't an accident?"

"Almost anything is possible. Wilson dies while he's leading a Buffalo Soldier troop. Winfield dies after he volunteers to replace Wilson with the Negro troop. I never have liked coincidences, Colonel. Not when men keep dying."

Roberts went to his window and looked out at the barren, dusty parade grounds on the western Kansas prairie. He shook his head. "Just ain't possible. That would mean we have a vicious, murdering gang among my officers. Don't seem possible."

"I'm probably wrong, Colonel. We'll wait and see what happens. We do know that somebody killed Winfield. Whoever it was will make a mistake and we'll nail the bastard."

"Oh, almost forgot. The womenfolk are having a social tonight, a little dance and a dinner at my quarters. Promptly at six or soon as the food is ready. We'll have about fifteen officers, Captains and above, mandatory attendance. When Marlene calls a social, everybody comes. Good food, three musicians, lots of frilly petticoats swirling and the tops of white breasts surging to get out. Welcome you to the post all proper."

"Much obliged. I'll be there."

Colt went back out to the parade grounds and walked across to the stables and the paddock. He checked the guard post and the spot where Lieutenant Winfield was found. Had to be, damn well had to be. Private Sapp was lying and laughing. How in hell could Colt make him tell the truth? He'd have to come up with some way, and damn fast or a killer would go free.

The social was the women's affair. Of the 40 officers on the post, only fourteen were married, and those happened to be all Captains and above, except one. First Lieutenant and Mrs. Wilbur Tryon were also invited.

The three musicians were enlisted and were paid two dollars each for performing. One played a fiddle, one a resurrected piano that had come across the plains in a wagon, and the third one a guitar.

The ladies had blossomed like peach trees in the spring, wearing their best dresses with flouncy sleeves, bustles and floor length skirts. There were three or four gowns deeply cut in front to show a swell of breasts. It always amazed Colt that the ladies buttoned their dresses up to their throats during the day and for church, but for a dance it was perfectly all right to push up their breasts with corsets so they could show a blush of white over a low cut gown.

He danced first with Marlene, the Colonel's lady. She had put on a few pounds since her last child and was pleasantly plump with massive breasts. He was sure her size, and the Colonel's general waistline, were a good indication that she was a fine cook.

"Welcome to Ft. Wallace," she said smiling. "I understand you're here to start a Lightning Troop. Here in Kansas that should be a real task."

They waltzed around the cleared living room and into the dining room of the Colonel's house. A detail of soldiers had moved all the furniture back and rolled up the carpets to make way for the dance.

"Ma'am, my real task is trying to remember how to waltz. I never could get my horse to do that three step."

Marlene laughed. "You are funny! I hope you stay around a while. So many new men come and go."

Colt let it pass, and managed to miss the other dancers as they waltzed around the two rooms. No more than half the people danced at a time, as if by mutual consent. That meant there was enough room.

Colt would much rather have been dancing with Doris back at Ft. Leavenworth, but that would have to wait.

He was kept constantly in motion by the women, all ready to have a new dancing partner after being in one fort for so long. Most of the officers assigned there were in place for what could be ten or twelve years.

The army had no policy of moving officers or men around unless a fort was closed, or the officer rated a new and better post due to a promotion. Some enlisted men were known to have served at only one fort or camp during their entire twenty years in the army.

Soon Colt danced with Bonnie Laughton.

She moved in closer than most of the women did so her breasts touched his chest. She looked up at him and smiled. She was a black eyed little redhead who seemed always to be in motion.

The musicians struck up a jig and Colt stood and watched while Bonnie did a spirited jig for them. Most watched. Then the music settled back to a two step and they all danced again.

"That was fancy footwork," Colt said.

Bonnie grinned. "Thank you, kind gentleman. You away from your wife?"

"Afraid so. She's in Leavenworth."

"A long time, I bet." Bonnie rubbed against him gently. "If you really get an urge, I mean nice ladies don't even suggest such a thing, but if you really get interested in some company, you just send me a note."

He looked down at her, surprised. She was one of the women with a low cut dress, a revealing red one, and fully half of both good breasts showed over the fabric.

"Now no high and mighty with me. I know how men think and what they need every so often. Some women need it too," she said quickly. "It ain't like it was something wrong, or anything. We're way out here in the middle of nowhere. I know my husband messes around now and then. We have this agreement, that if it's fine for him, it's fine for me. Does that shock you?"

Colt watched her pert face, then glanced to where their bodies met gently at their chests. He laughed softly. "Surprise, more I guess, than shock. Yes, surprise. You're a beautiful lady."

"So what's wrong with more than one man treating me like a lady . . . in any number of different positions?"

"Mrs. Laughton, I'm flattered, but I'm a one-woman man. And that woman is back at Leavenworth. I thank you for the dance."

He twirled her around to where they had started, bowed slightly and walked over to the punch bowl. It was a fruit punch with a chaser built in. He wasn't sure how strong the alcohol portion was. Colt took one more cup and watched the dancers.

While Colt sipped the punch, Captain Laughton danced with his wife and Colt could see them talking. Twice Laughton looked over at Colt with what he figured was surprise.

As the guest of honor, Colt had to be the

first to leave. He watched the people and at just before midnight, he kissed Marlene Roberts on the cheek, paid his respects to the Colonel, and walked out the front door toward his quarters.

It wasn't until he had stepped inside, lit the lamp and carried it into the small bedroom, that he realized he was not alone. Bonnie Laughton's bright red dress lay in a heap on the foot of the bed and she sat there naked and waiting for him. She held out her arms.

"Damn, I'm glad you finally got here," she said, standing and stretching.

Colt had seen it happen before. He grabbed her dress, pushed it against her chest, and pulled her toward the door.

"You've got thirty seconds to get into that dress, Bonnie. At the end of that time, whether you're dressed or not, I'm pushing you outside and then I'm locking the door."

"You wouldn't do that, Colonel. You want me." She pushed up and tried to kiss him, but he brushed her face away. She pressed her body against his, rubbing slowly.

"You have fifteen seconds," Colt snapped.

She jerked away, sliding the dress over her head without buttoning the bodice. She snorted and shook her fist at him as he pulled the door open. He watched her striding down the front of the long wooden building where the officers were housed. Two doors down, six men boiled out of a room and headed his way. They stopped quickly when they saw the woman coming toward them.

Colt hurried that way to identify the men, but they saw him coming and ran into the darkness. When he got there, only Bonnie remained.

"You'll never know what you missed out on tonight, Colt," she said. There were tears in her eyes. "They made me do it, my husband and the others."

"Who were they?" Colt asked.

She shook her head, slowly buttoned the fasteners up the front of her dress, and looked away. "Can't tell you that," she said softly. "I just can't tell you who they were. Bad enough you know that Victor was in on it. Makes me look like a real shit."

Colt didn't contradict her as she watched him a minute, then she turned and walked toward her quarters at the other end of the line of residences.

Colt went back to his rooms and closed and barred the door. The timing would have been right. The six men would have been into his room before he could have found his pants if he'd taken Bonnie up on her offer. He'd have been naked and all over the Captain's wife when Laughton and his witnesses charged into the room and Bonnie would have yelled rape. Then his value on the post as an investigator would have been reduced to zero.

Captain Laughton must be scared of what might turn up. He could be the man with the long knife!

IV

COLT HEARD THE news the next morning in the officer's mess.

"Damn near beat him to death," the Captain sitting across from Colt said. "Would have, I bet, if the interior guard hadn't run up and fired his rifle. That scared off them two jig-a-boos faster than butter in a hot skillet."

"There were witnesses, you say, and the two Negro troopers have been arrested and put in the stockade?" Colt asked.

"Not really, sir. Arrested and confined to quarters. We don't have a proper lock up here."

"But charges are being brought for a court martial?"

"I reckon, Colonel. Damn, I knew we'd just keep on having trouble with them damn nigras. Ain't right, them wearing the uniform."

"Abe Lincoln seemed to think it was a good idea, remember?"

"Hell, he's dead and gone. A lot of his fancy talk is dead and buried, too. This white boy was from the south. From what I hear, the two nigras wouldn't get out of the way when he wanted to walk past."

"Christ! He demanded they get off the walk or out of his way so he could walk past like a king or something? It's come to that." Colt snorted. "At least we've learned one thing."

"What's that, Colonel?"

"One white soldier shouldn't pick a fight with two Buffalo Pony Soldiers."

A half hour later, Colt stood in front of Colonel Roberts and frowned.

"I'd strongly suggest that those two men be put in protective custody somewhere, Colonel. The situation here could be described as explosive. You could have a full scale war right here in the camp if this isn't handled right."

"I'm trying to handle it the best way I can, Colonel," He walked around his desk, chewed on an unlit cigar. "All right, we'll use the old paymaster's office as our stockade. Place is built like a bank vault."

He called in his First Sergeant and gave the orders. Two men from the interior guard supernumerary would stand guard at the door of the office which was just down from the sutler's store.

Colonel Roberts looked back at Colt. "Now, I think it's past time that you tell me why you're here. Your orders said you were going to form a Lightning Company, but you don't seem too damn anxious to get started on that. Why did Phil Sheridan really send you in here? Bet Phil told you not to let me in on it."

"Fact is, Colonel, he said that was up to me. I think you should know. You're on his shit list. He says this is the worst post of any under his command. He wants things cleaned up or you get shipped out to the boondocks to a hard duty post."

"Goddamn!" Roberts rubbed his jaw and walked around his desk again. "At least you lay it on the line. Hell, what's first? I can't do anything about this black and white fight."

"You can keep a lid on it, keep the troops apart. I've got a suspicion we've got far bigger trouble than an occasional fight between the enlisted."

"What's that?"

"The Brotherhood."

Colt said it softly and Colonel Roberts's head snapped up, his eyes widened and he sat down suddenly in his chair.

"Where the hell you hear about that?"

"Around. What do you know about it?"

"Not enough. Damnit! Why did this have to develop on my post?" He pounded his fist on the desk top three times, then winced and looked up.

"You've got anything I know. I heard the whispers about six months ago. We had a brand new Second Lieutenant on the post who wanted us to treat all of the troops alike, joint barracks, drills, the whole thing. He turned into an obnoxious do-gooder. I had him transferred after three months.

"But already there was a group formed who called themselves the Brotherhood. Nobody knew who they were or what they did. But now and again, a Negro soldier would be pounded around if he got out of line on the white side of the fort.

"Two months ago, I had an officer come

in bitching about being given a bad time because he was the white leader of a Buffalo Soldier company. Hell, I assigned him to the job. He said he wanted out. I said tough shit. Most of them want out. That was his job. After a year I'd see if I could move him to a white company.

"Then he told me he'd been threatened by some other officers to quit the job as Company Commander of the black unit, or get his ass kicked and both arms broken. I called all of my officers together and explained the facts of the army today to them. This ain't the old army, this is the new army. We got Negro troops and we got to learn to live with them. Even the southerners. We've been assigned six Negro infantry companies and six Negro cavalry troops here. That's twelve officers I have to assign to black units.

"I laid it out. An assignment was made and would hold. If I heard any more harassment of commanders of the black units, I was going to bring half of the officers up on charges."

He walked to the window and came back. "So that settled things down for a while. Then Lieutenant Wilson died and now Winfield."

"Your pot is about to boil, Colonel Roberts. The enlisted don't figure in on this, so far. That fight with those two blacks and the white probably was a coincidence. Let's hope it stays that way. Let me tell you what happened last night after the party."

Colt told Colonel Roberts, who shook his head. "That Bonnie always has thrown her ass around a little. Discreetly. For a while she was waving it at me. Just as soon as her husband got his major's leaves, she was going to invite me to a party in her bedroom. Just her and me in our birthday suits. So Laughton must be our killer."

"Might be. Might not be. He's surely turning up in strange places, Colonel, I need three men, troopers assigned to me on detached duty. No questions."

"Fine. You want smart lads, or muscle men?"

"Smarter the better. Have them report to my quarters just after noon mess."

Colonel Roberts watched Colt. "Look, Harding, I don't want any more bodies showing up around here."

"Won't be. I aim to catch myself a killer, maybe a double killer, and get this fort back in Phil Sheridan's good graces. Don't worry, Colonel, you'll make general yet."

Colt went out and walked the fort. He hadn't done that before. The twelve black units were at the far end of the post, each group with a barracks of its own. The whole fort used the company cook style of army mess and he saw the cooks getting ready for the noon meal.

Beans, salt pork and maybe some bread and coffee. Army fare was about the same all over. He stood leaning against a barracks and watched the Negro Pony Soldiers go through their riding drills. Most posts had an hour-and-a-half a day horsemanship work, six days a week. Most troops needed it.

The average trooper had not even sat on a horse before he enlisted. Any riding skills had to be taught them by the army. Most cavalry units gave little riding training. The men simply picked up how to ride through experience and by making mistakes.

Colt watched the drills. In some cases, the officer stood or sat astride at one side and let the colored sergeants put the men through the drill. A few were handled by the white officer. One troop drilled faithfully without any white troop officer in sight.

The overall black and white problem wouldn't be settled on this fort, Colt was sure of that. It would take at least a hundred years for there to be any kind of equal treatment for blacks and whites, and maybe not even then. He was glad that wasn't his job. But the black/white problem seemed to be at the root of the trouble here at Ft. Wallace.

His immediate problem had to be solved quicker. He was anxious to get his three men and start them doing what he wanted to do.

First Lieutenant Leroy Roberts stood stiffly in front of his father's desk and saluted.

"Lieutenant Roberts reporting to the Commanding Officer as instructed, sir!"

"Leroy, I can see that," the Colonel said. He returned the salute, knowing his son would hold his until his father saluted. "Sit down, Leroy, for God's sake and act natural. I've got a small problem on the post and I want your help."

"Yes sir, whatever I can do."

First Lieutenant Leroy Roberts sat on the very front edge of the chair stiffly at attention. His eyes looked straight ahead.

"You hear a lot more talk among the officers than I do. They clam up when I come around. I want you to keep your ears open for me. Right now, what do you know about the Brotherhood?"

Leroy stiffened more and a quick shudder went down his back. "Nothing, sir."

"Don't give me that, Leroy. We've all heard about them. A group of maybe ten to twelve officers on this fort banded together for purposes of their own. I want to know what they're doing and who they are."

Leroy shook, then collapsed back in the chair, his chin quivering. Sweat broke out on his forehead and formed small drops. One ran down and dripped off his nose.

"Sir, that's all I've heard."

"Come on, Leroy. Your old man might be court martialed and kicked off this post if I don't get this cleared up. You know more than you're telling me. Talk, damn you!"

Leroy caught his breath and for a moment he nearly started sobbing. He beat back the gut urge and wiped his eyes.

"If . . . if I told you anything . . . I might get killed. You know what happened to Lieutenant Wilson and Winfield?"

"You're telling me both those men were murdered by the Brotherhood?"

"I can't say that for certain, sir. But the

talk by some of the officers is that's what happened."

"Who are these bastards?"

"I don't know."

"If you had to pick out three of them, who would you suspect, Leroy?"

"Oh, god, I'm a dead man!"

"I might kill you myself, Leroy! Who would you pick?"

Leroy wiped the sweat from his forehead, blew his nose, adjusted his shirt and then looked back at his father. He started once, then stopped. His hands moved around like wounded birds without a place to land.

"Captain Laughton, and Lieutenants Tryon and Zennican."

"Why those three?"

"They talk a lot. They are all bullies, mistreat their men, and all three have made terrible remarks about the Negro troopers."

"And about the white officers who have been assigned to command them?"

"Yes, sir."

"Do you think the Brotherhood is aimed solely at the blacks, and at whites who work with them?"

"Yes, sir."

Colonel Roberts made some notes on a

piece of paper on his desk, then watched his son.

"I've got a special assignment for you, Leroy. I want you to join the Brotherhood."

Lieutenant Roberts gasped. His eyes went wide and his face whitened. He leaned back slowly in the chair as if he might faint if he moved quickly.

"Yes, Leroy, join the Brotherhood and give me a report in writing every day about who you talk to, what is said, how you join, who is in it, the whole thing."

First Lieutenant Leroy Roberts shook in the chair. Tears slipped out of his eyes. He looked away. His hands gripped the arms of the chair until they went white with the strain. At last he turned toward his father. "No, sir. I can't do that."

"Why not, son?"

"If they found out I was a spy, they'd kill me."

"You've been in danger before, Leroy."

"I've also heard that you have to beat up a Negro soldier or kill one for your initiation. I . . . I couldn't do that."

"You could pretend to beat one up. We'll arrange with Doctor Judson to put him in the sick ward for a week."

"I don't know if they would accept me as a member."

"Why not? Just tell some jokes about stupid Negroes, and bitch about them being on base. It would be easy."

"Yes, but I've heard . . . never mind."

"Heard what, Leroy?"

"Some of them laugh at me because I'm not a good officer."

Colonel Roberts roared in anger. He threw the pencil he had been using across the room and Leroy winced. "Damnit boy, show them. Show the fucking bastards, damnit! Be a goddamn man! Show the murdering shit heads you can be as mean and rotten as they are." Colonel Roberts paced to the window and back, then again.

"Leroy, you do this, and we pull it off, and I'll send a note of commendation to the Department Headquarters and put you up for Captain."

"Oh, damn!" First Lieutenant Roberts had dreamed of being a Captain for three years. "I'll . . . I'll try it, sir. No promises, but I'll try."

"Yeah! Wonderful! Now that's my son! Have your company clerk put your report in a sealed envelope in his daily report marked to First Sergeant Clarnerlet's attention."

"Yes, sir. That won't draw any attention. I'll try it."

Colonel Roberts grinned and slapped his son on the shoulder. "If you try to salute before you leave, kid, I'll bust you one in the chops. Now get out of here and get me some names!"

Lieutenant Roberts grinned for a moment, but as he walked to the door he realized what he was going to try to do and his knees almost gave way. He kept his feet, didn't let his father see the terror that showed on his face, and went quickly out of the Commander's office and into the August morning, Kansas heat.

Christ! If he messed up just an inch, he was a dead man.

V

THE POKER GAME had been going for almost a year. They held it every Tuesday night at Captain Laughton's house. It was one of the best family quarters in the fort, and he got it because he had fixed it up when the previous officer had left. It was detached, had four bedrooms, a large living room and dining room, and a screened porch all across the front.

Captain Laughton, Lieutenants Tryon and Zennican, and Captain Oberholtzer had been playing for nickels and dimes since around eight o'clock. The other men in the Brotherhood drifted in just after midnight. They came in the back door and the front door, sliding in through unlit rooms so no one could say they saw a group assembling. Most of the men were unmarried.

Interior guards had been trained not to notice movements around the officer country.

The blinds had been drawn well before, and the lamps turned low. Captain Laughton found that the low lights with lots of shadows increased the men's sense of the dramatic. It caught their attention and somehow surged their anger.

The cards and chips had been stashed and Laughton brought out bottles of beer, peanuts and popcorn.

He stood before the dozen men and nodded. Then, as he usually did, he brought up some recent event or some black/white problem for the men to get worked up about. "So what the hell, we're not gonna let the nigras walk all over us? We gonna put the assholes down! What do you say?"

"Yeah, yeah, yeah!" the softly chanted chorus answered him.

"We're not going to let the nigras think they're real soldiers, no matter what has to be done. Even if you get assigned to be an officer over them, you won't give up. You'll do your job adequately, but no concessions, no friendliness, no compassion for the black bastards!"

"Yeah, yeah, yeah!"

"We got ourselves something to deal with here tonight. His name is Private Adolph Streib."

"Yeah, how is our boy?" a voice asked.

"Doing better. Doc Judson says he's out of danger and just needs time to heal himself. We got a little evening up to do about this matter. After all, Private Streib is a white man!"

"Yeah, yeah, yeah!"

"Captain O, those two jig-a-boos have been stashed away in the old paymaster's office, right?"

"Yeah, using it as a real lockdown. But the lock isn't much better than any of the others."

"We got a man on as Sergeant of the

Guard who we can trust?" Captain Laughton asked.

He heard an affirmative answer.

"I'll need some volunteers."

Hands went up. He chose three and thanked the rest.

"You three stay here after the meeting. We'll go on a little walk."

Everyone laughed.

"Now, I suggest that any of you who are Company or Troop Commanders for the Negro outfits, start putting pressure on the Adjutant for a change of command. If six or eight come in one after another, the brass will start getting the idea. If no officer will lead those twelve units, what the hell good are they to the army?"

They talked up the idea for ten minutes. At the end of it, the three men who had been assigned against their wills to the infantry section of the Buffalo Soldiers, agreed to launch a move for a new assignment the next day.

"We have a new member tonight. You all know him. First Lieutenant Herman Adams. He's been on post for about six months, comes from Illinois, and did two years at Ft. Phil Kearny so he's drawn his share of Indian blood and is a damned good man!"

The ritual of the new member began. He gave a speech about his early life, his likes, wants. Then he told about his first sexual encounter to the hoots and hurrahs of the men. Then he told them for fifteen minutes why he hated the Negroes and how he was firmly committed to getting them out of the U.S. Army, which was his profession and his life for the past five years.

"Our membership committee has investigated Lieutenant Adams, and found him eminently qualified to join us," Captain Laughton said.

"What about his initiation?" a voice asked from the shadows.

Captain Laughton laughed. "Oh, yes, we've thought of that. Lieutenant Adams will be the fifth member of our little detail tonight to the paymaster's office."

They broke up then, the men talking, trading jokes about Negroes and poor white trash, and then they drifted off, singly so they wouldn't be noticed.

Captain Laughton moved his four men out to a small shop in back of the house where each picked up a short piece of iron pipe and a half-inch rope.

"We'll make them spooks think we're gonna hang them!" Captain Laughton said.

Five minutes later, Captain Laughton came up behind the two guards near the door of the old paymaster's lock room. He clubbed one guard who went down with a sigh. Before the other could turn around and look, the .44 pistol muzzle pushed into his neck.

"Move," Laughton said.

He walked the guard into the darker shadows and whacked him along the side of the head just hard enough to knock him senseless.

Back at the paymaster's, the four officers had pulled on jackets to hide their rank and lifted neckerchiefs to cover their faces. Then they pried the lock off the door and the two frightened black men were roughly dragged out. They walked them a quarter-of-a-mile into the plains, off the military post, then began systematically beating them. They used the pipes first, then with the two Negro soldiers battered and helpless, the five officers worked with their fists and boots.

Neither black man said a word. They knew anything they said would only make their suffering greater.

Lieutenant Adams swore and kicked one of the men who fell down. He stomped on the man's forearm until he heard the bones break, then grunted in satisfaction.

"Which one?" Adams asked.

"What do you mean?" Laughton asked him.

"Which one is going to die?"

Laughton shook his head. "No. We've stirred up things enough. Neither one dies. That would be more than even a desk soldier like Colonel Roberts could take. Just mash them up good. They can't identify any of us.

"Besides, these two watermelon snappers will be too shit-scared to even admit they saw any human being out here tonight. So, boys, have fun, but don't kill the assholes, you all understand?"

The next morning, Colonel Colt Harding talked to Colonel Roberts about Lightning.

"I disapprove of your pulling in men from several companies. Breaks up the continuity of the troop or company unit. You know how the army has been, a trooper can stay in the same outfit until he's discharged."

Colonel Roberts swatted a fly that lit on his desk.

"No, on my command I want you to pick out the best of the Pony Soldiers as a troop and take the whole troop. I don't want a lot of shifting around."

"Colonel, it's your fort. I can't promise results like they should be with hand picked men, but we'll do what we can. I'll review the troops at midday parade and make my selection this afternoon. Can you arrange that?"

The Fort Commander called in his First Sergeant and gave him the orders for the parade of the horse soldiers.

Then he paused. "Now, Sergeant, you mentioned there was a small problem last night."

"Yes, sir. The two Negro troopers in the paymaster's office were spirited away and beaten severely. A detail found them about an hour ago. They're both still alive and under Doctor Judson's care."

"Thank you Clarnerlet, that will be all."

When the door closed, Roberts slammed his palm down on the desk. "The bastards! They've hit me again!"

Colt visited the two beaten men. Both had bandages on their heads and faces. One had a broken arm, the other a broken leg and both had internal injuries the doctor wasn't even trying to treat.

"I'm not set up to perform that kind of

surgery," he explained. "I'd wind up doing more damage than good. You want to talk to them?"

They were in beds in another room. A black orderly left the room when Colt entered.

"Morning, men. Looks like you got the worst of it this time."

Neither man said a word. One looked at Colt, then at his shoulder insignia, and turned to the wall.

"I'm here to find out what happened. I can't do a damn thing if you men won't talk to me. Did you recognize any of the ones who beat you?"

There was no reaction.

"Tell me this. It was dark, but there was some light." He pointed to the yellow stripe up his officer trousers through the blue cloth. "Did the men who beat you have this stripe up their pant legs?"

"Damn right they did!" the larger man said. "They was officers. White officers."

"Did they wear masks?"

The same man nodded.

"Could you recognize any of them? Even one? Had you heard any of the voices before?"

"Didn't talk much," the same man said.

He had the broken leg. "One said no nigger beats up a white boy and gets away with it."

Colt did what he could. He said the men who beat them would be found and court martialed. He was sincere. But when he left he realized he had no idea how to catch them.

He talked to Dr. Jay Judson again. "Anything you can tell me from the wounds? Weapons used?"

"Pistol barrels, maybe iron pipes . . . yes, iron pipes and fists and boots. What else did they need? A man with a broken leg and a bashed in face and torso can't fight too damn good."

Colt went back to the Commander's office and read the report of the Sergeant of the Guard.

At two-oh-one A.M. the Corporal of the Guard went to the paymaster's office special post to replace the two guards there. He found the on-site men both groggy, dazed and half unconscious. Both had been hit on the head sometime previously. Later they said they did not see who hit them.

At that time, it was determined that the prisoners were both missing and a limited search began. It concluded at daylight when the two men were found about five hundred yards north-

west of the fort limits in the prairie. Both had been beaten severely. One was unconscious. Neither could walk. They were transported to the fort physician and turned over to him.

The two men will be kept under guard in the infirmary.

Colt handed the report back to the First Sergeant without comment. The isolated incident had now been built into the main problem by the Brotherhood. Damnit!

Colt talked to the First Sergeant. "How many cavalry troops on the post?"

"Twelve, sir. Six white and six black."

"You know I have to pick one of the troops for the Lightning Troop. You've seen them ride, seen them in action, or at least reports of them in action. Which one, to your way of thinking, has the best leadership and performs the best in the field?"

"I can cut it to six in a rush, sir."

"How's that?"

"The Buffalo Soldiers are the best by far. The white troopers seem to be putting in their time. The Negroes have something to prove. They work harder, try harder, maintain discipline, have fewer casualties in action with the hostiles and generally fight with more guts and better than the whites."

"I'd heard that most of the blacks were

good fighters," Colt said. "You know what I have to do this afternoon?"

"Yes, sir. Good luck."

"Are you a betting man, Sergeant?"

"Time and again."

"You put the name of the troop you think I'll pick down on a piece of paper, seal it up in an envelope and give it to me. If you hit it, you win a five dollar prize."

"What if I lose?"

"Then I'll buy you a beer. Not a chance you can lose."

Colt took the envelope and folded it into his shirt pocket. Then he went out and stepped into the saddle of a mount the sergeant had arranged for him.

He had one of twelve units to pick. So far he had an open mind, but if the sergeant was right, he'd have only a one-out-of-six choice.

For a moment he wondered if the units not selected would be angry. Then he thought of the extra work the Lightning Troop would have and he decided after a week or so the other units would be glad they weren't selected.

He grinned, settled in the saddle and saw the troops riding into position on the parade grounds. Now this was part of his army duty he didn't mind at all: 600 men riding by and saluting him.

VI

COLT SALUTED SMARTLY as each officer brought his troop of cavalry past. He had instructed the First Sergeant to bring the white troops by first, then the Negroes.

As the first troop rode by in a four man front, as they would on the trail, he was not impressed. The men were not alert or sharp. Their lines were ragged of even the rows of four. By the time the last of the white troopers had paraded and returned to their mass position on the field, he felt the First Sergeant had struck the right chord about them—they were simply putting in their time, going through the motions.

Then the first troop, A, of the Tenth came. The guidon was held at the correct angle, the holder seemed excited about his job. The troops were better groomed, uniforms fit better, and they seemed to take a pride in their job as cavalrymen.

By the time all six of the Negro troops had paraded, he knew that the First Sergeant was right. He ordered the six white troops dismissed and they whooped as they left. Now he had the six black troops parade past in a column of twos. He left his parade position and rode beside and against the flow of the troopers, checking them critically, watching for horsemanship, attitude, even expression of the men.

After an hour more of parading, he dismissed all but Troop F and Troop A. He called the First Lieutenants in charge of the troops up to him.

"Gentlemen, do you know what we're doing here this afternoon?"

"No, sir," one officer said.

"Some kind of contest, I heard," the other man said.

"You're right, Lieutenant. It is a contest. I'm trying to pick the best cavalry troop on the post. Obviously, you two are the ones who are left for number one and two."

The officers both looked at each other and grinned.

"Tell me, do you enjoy your work? How is it working with these Negro troops? I'd like each of you to express himself to me about those two questions." He pointed to the shorter man to go first.

After two minutes of listening to the officer talk, Colt had a cold feeling about the man. He didn't speak with conviction. His comments about enjoying the troops and the duty fell thin and strained.

The second man was the opposite. He was honest, straightforward. He said he had resisted the assignment at first, but now he knew his men were some of the best fighters on the post. He considered going into battle with them was much safer than with a white troop. He said now if he was taken off his current assignment he would be unhappy.

Colt sent the men through a complicated drill technique that he knew they practiced by the hour on the parade ground. At the end of it he called the officers back.

"Gentlemen, in the past I've taken cavalrymen from various troops and formed what we call a Lightning Troop."

He saw the men's brows lift. They had heard of the troop.

"What we're doing here is forming a Lightning Troop in Ft. Wallace. Colonel Roberts decided that an existing entire troop would be used, not volunteers from all troops and companies.

"What we're talking about is a lot of work, a lot of training, and it's going to take guts and determination to make it work.

Now it's my responsibility to ask both of you if you would have any objections to taking on this extra work?"

Both said they would not, but he caught a gleam of anticipation in the man's eye who had impressed him before. He sent them back to their troops, then the First Sergeant rode out and dismissed the A Troop. Colt rode in front of F Troop and took the Lieutenant's salute.

"Congratulations, Lieutenant Phillips, your troop has been selected to be converted into Ft. Wallace's Lightning Troop."

"Thank you, sir. Would you like to tell my men what is happening and how it will work? I always like to get them in on the operation and planning as quickly as I can."

Colt's brows lifted. He hadn't heard talk like that since he'd been a Troop Commander. He grinned.

"Phillips, I'd be delighted to talk to your men."

Lieutenant Phillips spoke to his men a moment.

"We have just been selected as the best damn cavalry troop on Ft. Wallace!"

The troops cheered.

"That's bragging rights, but it also is going to mean some extra work. We've been designated to go into training as a Lightning Troop. I'm not sure what that entails, but I've heard it means a fast striking, lightly equipped force that can travel quickly and hit hard.

"The man who originated the idea and formed the first Lightning Troop, way down in Texas, will be training us. Right now he'd like to talk to you. Men, here is Lieutenant Colonel Colt Harding."

Colt rode up, asked the men to close in around him so they could hear better, and then told them about Lightning. He hinted at some of the training they would do, said that they would have more rifle target practice than they had done in all their lives before this, and that they would learn to ride like circus performers and out-ride the Comanches and Sioux.

"It will be tough, it will mean a lot of extra work, and when we're trained it will mean more than usual contact with the hostiles. But it will also mean you'll be one of the best fighting forces the world has ever seen."

From the looks on the black faces the men were enthused about the idea. But he wasn't putting it up to a vote. He turned the troop back to their Lieutenant and took the young man's salute.

"I'd like to see you in my quarters at one o'clock this afternoon, Phillips. Bring your three top enlisted men with you."

Colt turned and rode back to his quarters where a man took his horse and returned it to the paddock.

In his quarters, Colt wrote out a list of training activities for the troops to begin. The first would be a mile run, a jog, really. He wanted to see what kind of condition the men were in. The sergeants and Lieutenant Phillips would make the run as well.

He looked at his army issue boots. They were ankle boots which he wore inside his trousers as most officers and enlisted men did. Two good features were wide solid heels and square toes. They were fine for running. The men could have no complaint there.

By the time the three sergeants from F troop arrived with Lieutenant Phillips, the three trooper detail he had asked for was also there. He told the three privates to wait outside until he called them.

Colt brought the other four men into his quarters and found chairs and boxes for them to sit on.

"This is your first look at the Lightning Troop, gentlemen. It's going to be different, simpler, easier. Briefly, when we hit the field for a hundred and twenty mile ride, for example, we will take no wagons, we will take few supplies. We will live off the land and we will not have a bugler along. The idea is to move light and to move fast.

"Sixty miles a day will be a light day. You'll have more rifle and pistol range work than ninety-five percent of the army, and you'll get so you can hit what you aim at.

"I've worked out a list of projects for you, including working on your equipment. All equipment not on the list will be turned in to your company supply room and stored.

"Tomorrow morning at five-thirty the troop will form up outside my office on foot. Your training will start then. This afternoon I want you to strip down your gear to the minimum specified on this list. Sergeants will see that everyone in the troop is ready for inspection on the new equipment list including saddle, blankets and all gear for the trail, by noon tomorrow."

He watched the men looking at the equipment list. "Right, no sabers, they never were any good. Right, twice the usual issue of ammunition."

"Lieutenant Phillips, how many of your men have the Spencer repeating rifle?"

"Maybe six or eight in the whole troop, sir."

"I'll give you an order to take to the fort supply room. I want every man in your troop equipped with a Spencer within a week, if we have to take them away from the officers and non combat personnel."

He saw the surprised, pleased looks from the sergeants. "One more thing. We'll be having some physical training, a lot of horsemanship training, and unarmed combat as well as target practice. Officers and sergeants will be expected to participate in all of these activities. And everyone must qualify in each category to stay in the troop.

"Sergeants, do you understand what I'm saying?"

"Yes, sir!" they all said almost in unison.

'Take that list and get busy on equipment." The sergeants saluted and left.

Lieutenant Phillips watched Colt for a moment. "Sir, you mean I'm going to do the training with the men?"

Colt laughed. "No, Lieutenant, not 'do' the training. You'll be leading it, instructing, you'll be better at it than any man in your command.

"For starters, tomorrow morning we'll be going on a mile run. I hope you're in good physical condition. If not, you'll be training up to it with your men."

"A mile?" Lieutenant Phillips shook his head. "I can't even remember the last time I walked a mile." He shrugged. "Hell, it'll be good for me."

"We'll have special training every morning, go on special training rides every afternoon. No more drills, we'll be getting ready for the real thing."

"You mentioned hand-to-hand fighting. Who will be our instructors?"

"There is a small village of friendly Arapaho just outside the fort who are used as hired scouts, is this correct?"

"Yes, sir. We have about fifteen of the better trackers on the payroll."

"Those same scouts will be used as instructors for hand-to-hand fighting. How better to get ready to kill an Indian with a knife, than to have an Indian show you how they will try to kill you? We'll use wooden knives at first."

"About the ammunition for target practice? It's been the Commander's policy to charge all troop commanders for rounds used for purely target practice."

"Yes, I've run into this before. The next supply train coming to the fort will have ten thousand rounds in my name to be used by the Lightning Troop. This is a direct allocation with General Phil Sheridan's blessing. Nobody will argue with that. Most of it will be expended to teach our men how to use their rifles to hit what they aim at—the first time.

Lieutenant Phillips grinned as he stood. "My God, I've died and gone to heaven! I can't believe this."

"It's all true. And remember, you're going to have to take over this operation when I leave. Which could be at almost any time. I'll have a complete training schedule worked out for you. It will take at least four or five months. It includes tracking, and living off the land taught by our Arapaho friends and riding off your horse to one side and shooting under your mount's neck the way the good Plains Indians do. Have you seen them do that, Lieutenant?"

"Yes, sir. That kind of riding almost got me killed."

"Next time Indians do that to you, simply shoot the Indian war pony in the head and then kill the Indian when he scrambles out of the dirt."

Colt watched the young man glowing. It was a joy to see his excitement. "Oh, Phillips. One more thing. Nothing that we've said here is to be repeated to anyone in the officer corps. We'll surprise them. Also, I don't want the men to know about the little run in the morning until I tell them, understood?"

"Yes, sir."

"All right, Phillips, get with your men and see that their equipment is squared away. For tomorrow they bring no weapons, no hats, no gear. Just boots, pants and shirts."

"We'll be there."

"Get out of here, Phillips," Colt said and waved when the officer saluted.

He called in the three enlisted men. For ten minutes they talked. He found out their names, where they were from, how long they had been in the service, got them relaxed. One had two years of college and enlisted in the Army when he ran out of money. Another had been on a farm in Iowa, and the third was from the streets of New York City.

He instructed them carefully what they should do. One was assigned to shadow Captain Laughton.

"I want a written report from you every morning what the Captain did the preceding 24 hours. You might not get to sleep in your bunk for a while, but this is important. If he talks to someone you don't know, try to find out who it is. I want to know when he goes to the crapper and if he's making love to his wife. Everything! Now get a small pad of paper, a pencil from the First Sergeant at the Commander's headquarters and get to work. Your job is to stay out of sight, not to let him ever see you. If a non com questions you, show him this piece of paper."

Colt had written a short note to the effect that this named soldier was on temporary duty assigned to Lt. Col. Colt Harding and he should not be ordered or directed or interfered with.

He gave a copy of the note to each of them. "Use that only if you have to.

"Starting now, you're on eight hour shifts. Work out between yourselves when and where you relieve each other. It's like an eight hour guard duty tour. One of you find the Captain and get on the job right now. He'll most usually be at his company headquarters office, at his house, or somewhere in between. Work it out among yourselves."

He pointed at one. "You and I want to go check with First Sergeant Clarnerlet at the Commander's office and find out which horse has been assigned to me. Go down to the stables and groom her and get her ready for a ride this afternoon. Have her here at two-thirty sharp."

When they left, Colt took out pen and paper and wrote his wife, Doris, a letter. It had been too long since he had seen her. For a moment he thought of the naked, delightful form of Bonnie Laughton. What a roll on a mattress she would be. But he remembered Doris and knew that she was much better in bed than Bonnie could possibly be. He had to get this mess cleaned up here and head home to Ft. Leavenworth.

VII

IT WASN'T COMPLETELY light when Troop F assembled in front of the flag pole on the parade grounds the next morning at 5 A.M. Colt made sure he was up and dressed and ready for the run. He went out hatless, wearing his two-inch wide leather belt, but he detached the holster and left his Colt six-gun in his quarters.

He took the troop report from Lieutenant Phillips, then spoke to the troops in their ranks of fours.

"The first thing we're going to do with this Lightning Troop is see how good your physical condition is. We start that this morning with a two mile run."

Colt paused for the expected groans and wails but heard nothing. Good.

"Don't worry. I'll be leading you, and Lieutenant Phillips will be right beside me. In Lightning Troop the officers and non commissioned officers never ask one of you to do something that they can't or haven't done. All of your sergeants and non coms will be running along with us."

He turned to the troop's commander. "Any time you're ready, Lieutenant."

Colt did a left face and began jogging away from them. Lieutenant Phillips got the troop into motion quickly and he fell in beside the Colonel.

"You don't believe in wasting a lot of time, do you, Colonel?"

"Hell no. I'm over thirty. I might only have another seventy or eighty years to get everything done I've planned."

They laughed, then settled down to an easy pace, one that Colt hoped the men could keep up. It was a little slower than the Indian trot. The Apache and Comanche could run this way for six hours without stopping, then be ready to go on the attack.

"Any idea where we run to cover two miles around here?" Colt asked.

Lieutenant Phillips grinned. "I was hoping you'd ask me. That way I can cut it down to a mile and a half." He took a deep breath. "All the way around the outside of the fort buildings is about three-quarters of a mile. We do it twice and a half, we'll be close."

They did. Everyone made it the first lap. Three men fell out on the second round and another six fell into the Kansas dust before they came back to the flag pole. The pace had held up fairly well, but Colt had tired and let it lag a little after the second circle of the camp.

As the stragglers struggled into the formation, Colt waited for the company report.

"We still have two men unaccounted for, sir. I'll send a party out looking for them. Any new orders?"

"Back to your barracks and work on equipment. I'll inspect it just after noon mess, then we'll start our mounted training.

I want every man in the saddle. How many in your troop now, Phillips?"

"Forty six, sir. I'm next on the list for the first four Negro replacements who arrive."

"Carry on."

Colt walked over to the Fort Commander's office and found him ready to talk.

"I had three officers this morning request transfer from their duties as Company or Troop Commanders with the Negro units. They all gave the same reasons, which sounded like they had been rehearsed."

"What did you tell them?"

"That this wasn't a volunteer job. They had been assigned to the post and they either did the job or face a court martial. They all said 'Yes, sir,' and went back to work."

"Does three in one morning sound strange to you, Colonel?"

"Damn strange, like somebody nagged them into doing it."

"Like the damned Brotherhood."

"Bastards! Wait until we bust them. I'll court martial any man I find who violated any regulations. Do it in a minute."

"Hope we have the chance. I'm getting the Lightning Troop moving. It's Troop F, in case you haven't heard. I like this Phillips, he has a good feeling for his men, they have a fine attitude, and Phillips maintains excellent discipline."

"What if some of the men in there don't measure up? I've heard you have tests and training and a lot of tough things."

"If enough men don't qualify, I or Lt. Phillips will ask for some transfers of volunteers from other Negro troops. It probably will be necessary."

Colonel Roberts squirmed a moment. "Hell, I guess it can't hurt anything. Most of them probably won't sign over anyway."

The Colonel found something on his desk. "I got this from Sgt. Clarnerlet. It's got your name on it."

Colt took the envelope and tore it open. It was his report from his round-the-clock watch on Captain Laughton. It was written in a fine hand telling what Laughton did during the day and evening. It all looked routine. He was not seen talking with any enlisted men, spent his day at his company headquarters, and watched his infantry men in a marching drill.

"Something important?" Colonel Roberts asked.

"No, not this time. I'll be getting one of

these each day for a while hoping it will develop into something."

"You don't want to tell me about it?" Roberts asked.

"Nothing to tell right now. Oh, those Indians outside of the fort, Arapahoes I heard?"

"Right. We use them sometimes for scouts."

"Good, when the Lightning Troop gets further into training, I'll be needing six or eight of them to help us on tracking, hand-to-hand knife fighting, and living off the land. Can your budget stand that?"

"We have a dozen on monthly pay. Help yourself." He frowned. "What kind of training? Tracking, knife fighting?"

"Yes, sir. Who better to train a soldier on how to fight against an Indian with a knife, than another Indian?"

Colt left the Colonel and felt frustrated as he stomped out to the wooden porch. He looked at the sprawling clapboard buildings that made up the Kansas plains army installation. A trap would be great for the Brotherhood, but he had no idea how to set one, or what to use as bait.

He had to get the Lightning Troop training started and at the same time get the fort "cleaned up" as General Sheridan called it. He had a suspicion that the Brotherhood was behind the worst of the problems here. If he could crack that bunch wide open, the rest of the situations would resolve themselves, or at least be less explosive.

First he had to find out which officers were in the Brotherhood. Yeah, that was all.

Behind Colt in the Fort Commander's office, Colonel Roberts paced to the window and back to his desk. He had sent for his son a half hour ago. Where was that kid? Someone knocked on the door and it opened. Leroy Roberts hurried in.

"Son, if you salute, I'm gonna whip your ass. Sit down and relax, this isn't a formal meeting. When the hell you gonna get married and provide your mother with a couple or three grandchildren?"

Leroy did relax then. He had been afraid his father would start in on the Brotherhood thing again. But it was just the old get married shoe.

"Like where around here am I supposed to find an eligible girl to marry? There isn't a town with a single woman in it within fifty miles of here."

"Yeah, I know. But you did have your

chances when we were stationed at Leavenworth. Lots of pretty young things running around back there."

"Most of them were ugly as a brick shit house."

Colonel Roberts laughed. "Yeah, true, but that one General's daughter had eyes for you. You ever stick it in her?"

"Not a chance. Then she would have trapped me saying she was pregnant."

"Probably. More women get married that way than we realize." The Colonel turned and frowned at his only son. "You do like women, don't you? I mean . . . remember that time I caught you pounding off your meat in the outhouse?"

"I'm not a homosexual, father, if that's what you're asking me."

"Damn good thing. Army goes crazy about that sort of thing. Seen two good officers sacked because they ass-fucked some pansy boys in their outfit. Damned convenient for them, but their butts burned in prison for ten years."

Colonel Roberts opened a tin of horehound candy and passed it on to his son who tossed a piece in the air and caught it in his mouth.

"You can still do that," his father said.

"Real talent shows through."

"How the hell you doing on the Brotherhood thing?"

"You only told me about it yesterday. I can't just blunder in and be obvious about it. I have to pick out the right man and then be subtle. They might not pay any attention to me. I do have a certain stigma because my last name is Roberts."

"Hell with that. Get the job done, subtle or flagrant. I need some answers or I'm down south commanding a half dozen army levee workers somewhere."

"I'm trying. I talked with Lieutenant Bartlett for an hour yesterday. We talked about the blacks. I gave him the idea I'd as soon shit on them as walk over them. So far it hasn't got me an invitation to any meeting."

"Keep trying. Got a letter from your grandmother in Boston. Your mother and I both read it. You answer it this time. Carry it when you leave so anyone who is interested will see it. Oh, thought I should tell you, we're getting in three new laundry women next week on the supply train. One of them is a little redhead, I hear. You might want to check them out first night they get in."

"Why not? Give me a call as soon as they arrive. I could do with some home cooking. That officer mess food is terrible."

"All the army food is terrible. Not even much game around here unless you like rabbit. Thanks for coming by, and don't salute. Good luck on your project, Leroy."

Lieutenant Roberts marched out of the office back toward his quarters. He curled into a ball on his bed and sobbed. He was not a homosexual, he was not! But he'd been afraid that he was for years. He'd never touched a man sexually. He'd had flings with girls when he was growing up. He remembered petting a girl's breasts and climaxing in her hand once when he was just a kid. He had loved it! But then after a baseball game at school he saw the other boys in the shower and he had to turn to the wall and climax right there! Was he a homosexual or not!

He'd been torn into pieces about that question for years. Twice he'd tried to make love to a woman and both times he couldn't even get hard. He had tried, she had tried, finally they gave up.

Now he was afraid to try. The last woman had laughed at him, made fun of him, and that had hurt more than anything. He didn't know. What was he, only half a man? How could he command troops when he wasn't sure he was a real man? For a moment he wished he was with that girl, Betsy, back in higher school when she had let him play with her breasts. It had felt so *good!* What the hell was he supposed to do now?

At last he sat up. He combed his hair, straightened his uniform and slipped on his campaign hat. He had a company to run, a good company. They would have dismounted drill in half an hour. He would be there to observe and to lead them. At least that was one thing he was good at.

On his way across the parade grounds to his company headquarters, Leroy Roberts found Lieutenant Bartlett falling into stride with him.

"Talking to the old man?" he asked.

"Yeah. Got a letter from my grandmother in Boston. He passes them on to me, then I have to answer." He took it out and shook his head. "Four pages and she'll have a dozen questions on each one. There goes my evening."

Bartlett walked a few steps without replying, then he looked up. "You really want to have some fun tonight, I got a suggestion. A few of us are going to have a "talk" with one of the black asses from Baker company. His C.O. says he needs some disciplining. From what you said the other night, thought you might be interested in coming along."

Bartlett continued, "Hey, it ain't that we gonna put him in the fort hospital or anything. Just kind of push him around a little and instill some army discipline in his black hide. Want to come?"

From the second it shaped up as an attack on a Negro soldier, Leroy Roberts had been steeling himself to make a decision. The lie came quickly. "Hell, yes! Count me in. When and where?"

"I'll stop by for you just after mess. Around six-thirty somewhere. We can't let it get too damn dark, we might miss that jig-a-boo." He laughed as he walked away toward his own company office.

Lieutenant Roberts watched him stride up the dusty street. Christ, it had happened. The first hint at a shot at getting into the Brotherhood. This could be a test, a proving ground. If he went, he would see who else was there. Half of them could be hangers on, or potentials like him. How did he pick them out?

If he didn't go, he would probably never have another chance to do what he had to do to save his father's army career. Christ! What a mess. His own army career was not important, but his father would be devastated if he never made General.

Damn! What the hell was he going to do come six-thirty?

VIII

COLT FELT UNEASY as he worked with the Negro men in F Troop that afternoon. They were better horsemen than some he had seen, but a dozen or so would need special riding training and practice. He pointed out the men to Lieutenant Phillips who promptly assigned them to special riding work with his best sergeant.

He wasn't uneasy about the new Lightning Troop. From what he had seen so far, they would round out into as good a unit as he had trained—if he had time to finish the training. He was becoming more concerned about the Brotherhood. How could he tie down names of the participants. He thought of one way he hadn't wanted to use yet, but decided it was about time.

Late that afternoon, Colt summoned a white soldier to his quarters and left him standing ramrod straight as Colt brewed a cup of coffee on his small wood cooking stove.

"Why did you get busted from Sergeant, Private Sapp?" Colt asked suddenly.

"No fault of mine, sir. Squabble between a Captain and a Major. I was the one took the blame, as usual."

"By that you mean the enlisted always catch the shit when it flies?"

"About right, sir."

"Except when you latch onto a Captain who will protect you. Like now."

"Don't rightly know what you mean, sir."

Sapp stood straight, only his eyes moved as his gaze followed the light Colonel.

"You know damn well what I mean, soldier. How long you been in the army?"

"Fourteen years, sir."

"What went wrong?"

"That's a personal matter, sir."

"Sapp, I'm charging you with the murder of Lieutenant Winfield. Your trial will be next week."

"What?"

"Murder in the first degree, as the civilians would say. The deliberate, brutal, torture killing of Lieutenant Paul Winfield."

"You trying to scare me?"

"No. I'm charging you with murder. You swore that you were at your paddock post every moment from ten P.M. until twelve-oh-one A.M. the night the officer was killed. That means you either saw him killed in the paddock, or you saw the men who did it, bring his body and drive the horses over it so it would look like an accident.

"All I want is a conviction. I'd just as soon hang you as the men who actually did it. It doesn't matter that much to me at this point."

"Son of a bitch!"

"Private, I missed what you said," Colt snapped.

"I didn't kill him."

"So, you now say that the man was in fact killed—murdered—and it was not an accident. We're making progress."

"Didn't say that, what I said was—"

"I heard you, Private. Was he killed there or somewhere else?"

"Christ, you could do it. You could put me in front of three officers on a court martial and they sure as hell gonna stretch my neck. Shit! This wasn't no way supposed to happen."

"The Captain said it would be safe for you, did he? I see by the guard records that you changed places with the man who was first scheduled to take the paddock post. You were put in at the last minute by a Sergeant Greggory."

"Yeah, so what? Happens all the time. I was supernumerary that night."

"Until needed. Until the Captain sent word to put you in place."

Colt sipped the coffee.

Sapp started to sag.

"You're at attention, soldier!" Colt brayed.

Sapp straightened, his scowl deepened.

"I figure you have about a month to live, with a review and all. Not a hell of a lot of time, is it, Sapp?"

"I didn't kill nobody."

"This time. The court martial couldn't agree the last time. About eight months ago, as I remember. Captain Laughton was your one witness. He saved your scalp by testifying for you. But not even the court martial board believed all that he said. You were asshole lucky, Sapp."

"I didn't kill the Lieutenant."

"Who did?"

Sapp turned and looked at Colt. "Sir, I don't know. That's the naked God's truth.

But I'm not gonna get hung to save some God damned . . ." He stopped.

"Some god damned *officer*, you were going to say. I don't blame you. I wouldn't either. To start getting that rope off your neck you better talk fast and loud. You answer my questions one by one, and you might not even be charged. Might not. Now, Private Sapp, who carried Lieutenant Winfield's body into the paddock?"

"Two men. It was dark."

"But you know who they were. Were they both officers?"

Sapp looked up quickly. "You know . . . Oh, damn. Yes, sir, Colonel, they was both officers."

"And you know the names of those two officers? You saw them and can positively identify them?"

Sapp looked at the ceiling, then down at the floor.

"At ease, soldier. Relax and think about what you're about to say. It could help you beat the charges, or it could throw you into a deep pit where the dogs will tear you to pieces."

Sapp sighed. "Oh, damn. They said they'd back me all the way, alibi me, the whole thing. Now I'm looking at a fucking murder charge. It ain't fair, goddamnit!"

"Life isn't fair, Private. The army sure as hell never said it was fair, especially to killers. Are you going to give me the names of those two officers, or do I put you in the stockade?"

"I'm a dead man either way. You get me, or they get me."

"They will never know."

"Damn wrong there, Colonel. Hell, they got people everywhere. My bet is they have somebody watching your front door. Somebody writing down the name of everyone who goes in and comes out of here. They know I'm here right about now."

"So hit back at them. Tell me the names."

"You give me your word as an officer I won't be charged?"

"Not with murder. Conspiracy, cover up, lying during an official inquiry, maybe. But you won't get hung for them. You testify the truth and the court will go easy on you."

"That's what they said last time."

"Captain Laughton told you that?"

Sapp's head snapped around suddenly. "Laughton. How the hell you know that?"

"I know a lot of things about you, Sapp.

A lot about the Brotherhood. Now the quicker you tell me what you know about that murder night, the better off you're going to be."

"Christ, I'm a dead man either way. I'll take my chances with you, Colonel."

"Who dumped the body?"

"Lieutenants Zennican and Bartlett. Neither one was good with horses and it took them twenty minutes to drive a herd over the body. You know how horses don't like to step on nothing."

"And you saw all of this and will testify in a court martial?"

"Damn right!"

"Can you write, Sapp?"

" 'Course."

Colt gave him a pad and pencil and told him to write down exactly what happened. "From the time the Sergeant of the Guard moved you into the list for the paddock guard post. I want his name and the times, everything."

It took Sapp a half hour to get it all down on paper. Colt had him sign on each of the four pages. As he finished and they went to the door there was a commotion outside.

Fifty white mounted men swung into the parade ground, formed up, and sat on their horses as if they had been on a several day's ride.

A sergeant hurried from the group to the Fort Commander's office and came back a moment later with Major Franke, the Adjutant.

Colt let Sapp slip out the door and into a knot of people who came out to see the visitor.

Five minutes later Major George Forsyth was ushered into Colt's quarters. Major Franke was with him.

"Colonel, Major Forsyth says he's got to talk to you, and since he needs quarters, figured you might like to share your spare room with him for a couple of days."

"Be glad to. George Forsyth?" Colt asked. "I've heard Phil Sheridan speak highly of you."

Forsyth grinned. "It must have been one of his good days." Forsyth slumped into a chair and waved at Franke. "Thanks, Major, I'll try to stay out of Colonel Harding's hair."

Franke left quickly and Forsyth closed his eyes for a moment. He was two or three years younger than Colt. He had thick brown hair and a round boyish face that hid his aggressive style.

Forsyth had enlisted in a Chicago regiment of dragoons in 1861 as a private and rose to the rank of Brevet Brigadier General during the Civil War. He had been a top aide of the Union hero of cavalry, General Philip Sheridan.

Now that Sheridan commanded the fourteen state and territory Military Division of the Missouri, Forsyth was again one of his aides. He had been reduced in rank to his permanent grade of Major in the drastic shrinking of the army after the war.

"Phil said I should find you here. I'm on my way to try to draw some blood from the savages who have been rampaging around this section of the country this summer. You've heard about the Sioux and Cheyenne raids that have burned whole settlements, cut up wagon trains, ranches and stage stations, and demolished the telegraph a dozen or more times? Well, the old man wants some blood. You know how the hostiles strike where they please and drift away. We try to chase them and they use back trail scouts to spot us. Then they break up into groups of twos and threes and fade into the hills somewhere."

Forsyth chuckled. "What am I doing, telling you how to fight Indians.

"We're expanding on your Lightning Troop idea. Setting up a roving Troop to move light and fast and hit the bastards where they live. So here I am. All Phil said was to make the bastards pay with some fresh red blood."

"Interesting assignment," Colt said. "Wish I had a Lightning Troop here to send along in support. But we just started training this one yesterday."

"We'll make out. I've got fifty men out there who need a couple of days of rest before we push on. Major Franke has put the troops up in the barracks and he's promised us some real good army food. I talked him into butchering a couple of local beef so my men can get some solid food."

"Where you heading, Forsyth?"

"Up north some and west. Might even get into Colorado Territory. I want to charge through the tributaries of the Republican River up in there. Know damned well that's where a lot of the warriors gallop off to after their murdering raids."

"Should be good hunting up in there, especially this time of year. They're thinking more about their winter's supply of buffalo jerky and pemmican than they are of war. The summer raiding should be about over."

"I've got fifty hand picked irregulars, and we've trained them up to fighting trim. Then too, we've got mostly Spencer repeating rifles. We can pour out a regular hellish hail of lead when we need to."

Colt poured him a cup of coffee.

"Oh, Phil sent along an envelope for you. That man writes more letters and orders than any General I've seen in this man's army."

Colt took the packet and put it on the table. He had enough problems right now without taking on any more.

They talked until mess call and went into the small officer's dining room. Forsyth knew three of the officers there. They shook hands and talked about old times. One of the men was Lieutenant Bartlett. Colt had not known much about him before. He was one of the two men named by Private Sapp as the ones who brought Winfield's body into the paddock.

The man was five-five or six, slight, with a drooping moustache and eyes that squinted as if he needed spectacles. He had a dark shadow of a beard and should shave twice a day to stay clean looking.

Colt left the men talking and slipped out of the mess. At the Commander's office he found his report from the watchers. Most of it was routine, but the last entry had been made late the night before.

Subject seen leaving his quarters just after midnight and moving to the stables and thence about fifty yards beyond the paddock into the prairie. There he met with three men who had already been in place. Could not determine who the men were, or where they came from.

Did discover that they were officers from the post when the meeting ended and all returned by different routes to officer country and quarters there.

What was Captain Laughton up to now?

IX

COLT SPENT THE rest of the evening with Major Forsyth. They played two games of chess, and worked on a half dozen bottles of beer Colt had brought from the sutler's store.

Then they told war stories about the conflict between the states, and finally fell into bed, half drunk and totally exhausted.

Lieutenant Leroy Roberts did not have such a pleasant evening. He met Lieutenant

Bartlett, as he had suggested, at the far end of the paddock. They were still in the fort boundaries but at the farthest point from any barracks or residences. The guard posted at the paddock could not see them.

For five minutes they sat on the ground waiting for the others. Six more men came, singly or in pairs. Roberts recognized some of them, but others hid their faces under the brims of their hats so they would not be identified.

Ten minutes later Captain Laughton and Lieutenant Adams walked up from the darkness leading a black corporal. His hands were bound together behind his back. They put the enlisted man in the center of the circle of officers and Adams spoke.

"Boy, you know why you're here?"

The black corporal from an infantry company rolled his eyes looking at the white officers and shook his head.

"No, suh. I surely don't."

Lieutenant Adams pounded his big fist into the Negro's side just over his kidney and the man went down in the dirt. He tried to lift his legs up to relieve the pain, but four men held him stretched flat on the ground.

Lieutenant Roberts touched Lieutenant

Bartlett's shoulder. "This isn't for me," he said. "I'm leaving."

Bartlett followed him twenty feet across the ground then stopped him.

"Roberts, we got ourselves a touchy situation here. What's going on over there ain't exactly according to army regulations. You said you wanted to come. Now you decide you don't want to participate. Some of our people are gonna think that's downright unfriendly."

"That's their problem, Bartlett, not mine. I just don't believe in ten men beating up on one."

"Maybe you'd like it one-on-one with me, right here, and right now," Bartlett said.

Bartlett was four inches shorter than Roberts and twenty pounds lighter.

"No. I have no argument with you. This type of . . . of action . . . is not my style."

"We still got our little problem. You're the Fort Commander's kid. You going to tell him what you saw tonight?"

"I have no reason to."

"We hear that you've said one word about this to anyone, and you'll be the next guest in the circle of friends out there. Do you understand what I'm saying, yellow belly?"

"There's no need . . ." Lieutenant Roberts started the words with anger, then stopped.

"Roberts, just remember the eleventh commandment: I swear that I will not bear witness against a fellow officer. Now get your prissy, yellow belly out of here. You're fouling the clean smelling, pure Kansas night air!"

Leroy Roberts had never been so angry in his adult life. He came within a fraction of a second of drawing his revolver and shooting the man in the heart. He was outraged. He was mortified. He was also terrified to think that he could almost take a fellow officer's life.

He spun on his toe and heel, doing a smart about face and walked back toward his quarters. Every second he thought he would feel a .44 round in his back. It didn't happen.

In his bachelor quarters, he brewed a cup of tea and drank it slowly. What was he going to do? He had tried to play the fearless he-man role for his father. He had failed miserably. He couldn't even stand to watch ten white men beating up a Negro.

For just a moment he wished he were back in higher school, living with his parents. He wished that the girl was there, the one who had let him play with her tits. Yes! He walked into his bedroom and stretched out on his back. His hands fell at his crotch as he thought about the girl. That had been the most wonderful afternoon of his whole life.

She had been so soft, so understanding. She said he could touch her, play with her, if she could play with his crotch. He hardly felt her opening his pants. Instead he had concentrated on unfastening buttons and lifting soft white cloth away. Then he saw them!

Her breasts were beautiful, soft and round and pointed with small red buds on the ends and round pink circles! He was mesmerized.

When he touched them he felt his hips jerk, and the girl yelped in surprise and then delight as he climaxed, his hips pounding a dozen times as she held his throbbing penis.

They had undressed each other and felt and fondled and played all that afternoon with things never seen before. Four times he had climaxed. It had been pure joy, total rapture. He never entered her but she had wanted him to.

Now on his lonely army post bed, Lieutenant Leroy Roberts rolled over on his stomach and relived that afternoon, climaxing into a towel and then throwing it across the room as he pulled his knees up toward his chin and sobbed for an hour.

The last thing he remembered thinking was what in the world was he going to do now. His father would demand a report. If he told the Fort Commander about the contact and the officers he recognized, the circle of anger, the Brotherhood, would come down on him—they would kill him.

A cold, numbing realization flooded through him. The Brotherhood would kill him the way they had Lieutenant Winfield. He sat up suddenly and screamed. Then he choked it off.

Either way he looked at it, Leroy Roberts knew that he was a dead man. It was just a matter of who was going to do the killing and how they did it. Mercifully, he at last drifted into sleep.

The next morning, Colonel Colt Harding took his F Troop Lightning men on a training ride. He moved them out quickly, raced along at seven miles an hour for the first six miles, slowed for a quarter of a mile walk, then charged along the next seven miles in an hour, and finally took a break.

He spoke to the three Arapaho scouts who came with them, and they grinned and faded into the plains. When they all met two hours later at a given bend in a small creek twenty miles from the fort, it was a little after ten o'clock in the morning.

The troopers had been instructed not to bring any rations. They looked at their sergeants and asked about food. The sergeants shrugged but soon asked Lieutenant Phillips. He asked Colt.

Harding called the men together. They had dismounted and cooled down their mounts and watered them. Now the black troopers gathered around.

"When we go on a 150 mile ride we don't want to be burdened down with a wagon or a lot of bad tasting army rations. So what we do is live off the land. Some of you know we had some Arapaho scouts along. Where did they go?"

The four scouts lifted up from behind a small rise of ground and walked forward. They carried ten jackrabbits and ten China pheasants.

"This is how we'll live off the land. You'll also learn how to be hunters on these trips, but for now you just get to be eaters. Who can eat half a jackrabbit?"

The critters were big, probably weighed out at four or five pounds cleaned.

"Watch how these men cook them," Colt said.

They crowded around as the Indians dug a trench in the bank of the stream and built a fire in it. The ditch was a foot deep and they laid out the fire along the twenty foot length. They burned the scrub growth and downed the dead brush along the banks of the stream, concentrating on drift wood that had caught on the small trees.

When there was a good bed of coals in the bottom of the ditch, they laid in the birds and rabbits. Both had been cleaned but not picked or skinned. They were rolled in a thick gooey mud made from the stream bed and when all were laid on the coals, the dirt was pushed back in until the rabbits and pheasants were entirely covered.

"In an hour that will be some of the best tasting meat you've ever eaten," Colt told them.

They put in an hour doing target practice. Each man had to put five rounds at fifty yards into a five inch bulls eye. About half of the men qualified and the others were given instructions in how to shoot lying down, in the seated position, and over a log.

When the target practice was over, they waited for the meat.

The Indians dug out the rabbits and pheasants, stripped off feathers and skin. Each man would get half a pheasant or a quarter of a rabbit. The man designated as company cook whacked the meat into chunks with his eight inch cleaver he had been instructed to bring along. Then the men ate. There were no complaints.

Lieutenant Phillips licked his fingers as he devoured his half a pheasant.

"Damn! Never knew pheasant could taste so good. Now the way I figure it, if we went out for three or four days, we could issue two days of rations per man to supplement our meat and eat better on the trail than we do in camp."

"About the size of it," Colt said. "I like the way your men are taking to the training. Have you had anyone ask to be transferred?"

"Only one. He's thirty-six years old and due to end his two year enlistment soon. He's actually too stove up to be riding at all. But the man is half heart and the rest guts."

They rode back without a break, averaging a little better than seven miles to the hour and pulled into Ft. Wallace tired, but to a man they were grinning ear to ear.

"Hey, we did twenty miles in under three hours!" Colt heard one jubilant trooper call to one of his friends in another company as the formation broke.

Yes, the men were going to make a fine Lightning Troop.

There was an envelope waiting for Colt when he checked with the fort First Sergeant. It was in a different handwriting from the others, but it was neat and easy to read.

The first two pages told of the routine goings and comings of Captain Laughton. Then with supper things changed.

Captain Laughton left by the rear door of his quarters, slipped from the house to the shed and waited for dusk. Then he walked by a roundabout way to Baker infantry company (Negro) and was met by an officer not identified. They both went to the back of the barracks where another white officer met them and gave them a Negro soldier with his hands tied behind his back.

Said soldier was marched and pushed into the night and soon brought to a location in back of the paddock and nearly off the fort limits. There were six or eight other men there. (Of-

ficers, we believe, due to the yellow trouser piping.) They began shouting at the Negro and beating him with their fists and feet. One officer was seen to leave when the beating began.

The affair lasted about twenty minutes, then the soldier was marched back to his unit. His hands were still tied He walked unsteadily, slowly. At the rear door he was untied and pushed inside the same barracks he was taken from.

Only two officers returned the soldier to his barracks. At that time Captain Laughton was lost in the darkness. He was picked up again a hundred yards from his home on the route he would have taken if he had come from the beating.

He went into his residence and remained there the rest of the night. There is some indication that both he and his wife were awake in their bedroom for about a half hour after he lit the lamp in said room when he arrived

Colt checked with the post surgeon but there had been no one treated that morning or afternoon for what could have been a beating. No Negro troops at all had been to see the medical man.

Back in the Fort Commander's office, Colt laid out his progress with the killings and reported the confession from Private Sapp and the naming of the two officers.

"Sir, my best judgment right now is to start a small war of my own, a war aimed at the nerves of one of these men. I want to let him know that I'm interested in his actions, his background, his daily activities, put him under a glass. What I'm hoping is that we can break one of the two and get some real confession about the deaths. Which man should I concentrate on?"

"Bartlett. He's small, has a moustache and a serious complex about his height. He's a good officer, but he's from a border state that has a lot of blacks. He must be seriously racially prejudiced. Yes, I'd think that Bartlett would be the man to break.

"Zennican is a tougher lot, rougher, silent, sullen sometimes, does not respond well to authority, and likes to run his company the way he wants to. Yes, go with Bartlett."

That evening, Colt read through the personal and military history file of Lieutenant Bartlett. Then he sent a message to the officer asking him to report to his quarters at 7:30 P.M. There was no reason given for the summons.

The officer knocked on Colt's door

promptly at 7:30. Colt had arranged for Major Forsyth to have dinner and spend the evening with Colonel Roberts.

Lieutenant Bartlett held his hat in his left hand and saluted smartly. "Lieutenant Bartlett reporting as ordered, sir!"

Colt walked back to the chair near the small kitchen table he had left to answer the door. He did not respond to the salute or the greeting. Let him sweat a little. Bartlett evidently realized he wouldn't get a return salute, and lowered his arm.

"Bartlett, I understand you're from Missouri."

"Yes, sir."

"Graduated from West Point in Sixty Four, so you saw some action in the war."

"Yes sir, eighteen months."

"Brevetted a Major during the war. Then when you elected to remain in the slimmed down army after the war, you went back to your permanent rank of Second Lieutenant."

"Yes, sir."

"Some companies and troops have two officers as I'm sure you know. We're going to be needing a second in command of the old F troop, that is now becoming Lightning Troop F. Would you be interested?"

"Why, it's an honor to be asked, sir. But I've been with my own troop for three years now. I'd hate to have to leave them. A lot of loyalty there. I know the men. We function well together."

"And the Lightning troopers are black. I understand, Lieutenant."

"That wasn't one of my reasons, sir."

"Would it be? Would you mind commanding a Negro troop?"

"No, sir. But not as second in command. I have my own troop now. It would be a demotion to go back to second."

"I see. What do you think of our Negro troopers, Lieutenant Bartlett?"

"Some are good, some are not so good. A lot like any unit in the army, I would imagine."

"What about discipline. Would you come down harder on a Negro troop than a white one for a similar infraction?"

"No, sir. No need to."

"That's strange, Lieutenant. I have it on good authority that a group of whites beat up a black soldier last night. He was being disciplined for something or other. That disturbs me, Lieutenant Bartlett. Disturbs me mightily."

Bartlett frowned as he heard the words.

He swallowed hard, then shrugged. "That does sound extreme. Discipline should be meted out within a company or troop to be effective."

"Then are you saying you don't approve of the whites beating up on the Negro last night?"

"It's not good discipline, sir. The matter should have been handled within the company. Peer pressure, sir. If the whole troop was given extra duty because one man got out of line . . ."

"I know about basic peer pressure, Lieutenant Bartlett. What I want to know is why did you participate in the beating of the Negro man last night?"

Sweat popped out on Bartlett's forehead where he still stood at attention.

"Sir. I . . . I did not participate. Last night I had a marathon chess game with Lieutenant Herbert Adams. He'll swear we were in my quarters from just after mess until well after midnight. If someone said I was at some beating, that person is lying."

"Actually it isn't one man, Lieutenant. The facts are I have three emisted men who saw the whole thing, followed some of the men back to quarters so they could positively identify them. We have those positive identifications. You were one of the men at the beating.

"So, knowing all of this, Lieutenant Bartlett, do you want to change your statement in any way?"

X

Lieutenant Ivan Bartlett frowned, then rubbed his face with his right hand and preened his moustache.

"You would take the word of an enlisted man rather than that of an officer? I say any man who accuses me of beating someone last night, or any night, is a liar. If there are three enlisted men who say that, there are three liars. If that is all, sir, I will be going."

"That's not all, Lieutenant!" His voice came sharply and Bartlett snapped back to attention.

"The three men I spoke of are working as special investigators for me. They are enlisted, and I trust them. A word of caution to you, Lieutenant. You are the only man on post besides the Commander who knows about these men. If anything should happen to them—any accident—if one of them stubs his toe or catches a cold, or gets the measles, I'm going to blame you and jump astride your skinny little neck with a noose and hang you high. Do you understand?"

"Yes, sir."

"I think you're the one lying here, Lieutenant. Those silver bars on your shoulder straps don't make you god, although some officers seem to think it does. If so, I'm a bigger god than you are. So you better be afraid of me, and pray that my three men don't so much as get a broken fingernail."

Colt stared at the man who held his gaze for a moment, then looked away.

"Now get out of here. You disgust me!"

Bartlett whirled and stormed out the door, but he closed it carefully.

Colt looked out the window a minute, then drew the blinds. He had been bluffing most of his accusations. But it had seemed to strike home. Colt had a strong feeling that Bartlett was one of the men at the beating last night, but he could not prove it. He could prove that Laughton was there and nine other officers.

Colt took out a sheet of paper and wrote a letter to Doris. It took his mind off the puzzle. That often helped. Tomorrow he would ask for four more men, two to trail

Bartlett around the clock and two on Zennican, just to see what developed.

A half hour after Bartlett left Colt's quarters, three men stood in the middle of the dark, deserted parade grounds. No one was within a hundred yards of them. No one could see them. They hardly could see each other.

"I agree, something has to be done about him," a heavy voice said. "He's coming too damn close."

"How could he know so much about last night?" another man said.

"It has to be soon," the third man with yellow piping down his pants legs said.

"Tomorrow. I'll take care of it, tomorrow. Don't worry. There's a training ride scheduled for F Troop at 5:30 in the morning. Lieutenant Colonel Colt Harding will come back from that ride dead over his saddle!"

"Make damn sure."

"It's going to cost a hundred dollars."

"Shit, I'll do it myself for that."

"No you won't, too dangerous. Something can always go wrong. We play it safe, by the numbers. Ten dollars each. I need the money by dawn."

"In advance?"

"Who knows how long a man who would shoot a Colonel might live afterwards?"

The three men hurried away into the night. They each had men to contact, money to collect.

Colt Harding led F Troop on the training ride a little after 5:30 A.M. heading south this time into new country for him. They rode for five miles, found a small ravine they could use as an impact area, and set up a fold out cardboard box as a target. Then they began firing at it from horseback while riding past.

After each man had fired seven rounds from his Spencer, Colt showed them again how to ride while hanging off the side of the saddle by the left stirrup and shooting his pistol under the mount's head. The troops hooted in delight as he hit the target four out of five shots from twenty feet.

He had the troopers ride by him one by one and study the way he hooked his left foot in the left stirrup after swinging it up on the seat of the saddle. He leaned down and kicked his right foot up on the mount's back as he pushed around the horse's neck and fired the pistol. When everyone had a close up look he stood in his stirrups.

"Now I want every man to try the same thing with your mount stopped. Do it now. I'll be watching. Sergeants, you do the drill, too."

Colt rode among the men, watching their first attempts. Some of them fell off and hit the ground. Others picked it up quickly.

Colt had Lieutenant Phillips try it first. He nearly fell, then got his balance and rode by and fired at the target. Then the three sergeants tried. They did it walking their mounts. The horses had some adjusting to do as well. After three walking attempts past the target, the sergeants were told to do it once more and this time to fire their pistols, all five rounds.

Two of the sergeants completed the run and one even hit the target. The third sergeant fell as he tried to fire. He swore, got back on, made another walk by and this time did it right and hit the target four out of five times.

The troops cheered.

Colt sat down in his saddle and directed the troopers to come by in their usual groupings and try the firing at any speed they wished.

He had just given the command and the first trooper went past the target when a heavier sound billowed through the Kansas autumn. A rifle ball took a patch of mane out of Colt's horse. He whirled to find the bushwhacker.

A tell tale blush of blue smoke rose from a small hillock three hundred yards away. Colt at once swung down on the off side of his mount and galloped toward the sniper. The surprise move had the desired effect and the gunman tried two more shots aiming just over the saddle but he had a small target, only one of Colt's legs and his boot in the stirrup.

Colt's horse covered the distance quickly to the pall of blue smoke, as two sergeants pounded along following him. Colt lifted over the rise and spotted the gunman trying to mount his horse. Three rounds from Colt's reloaded revolver stopped the man. He took a round in the shoulder and a second high up through his chest. The force slammed him off the horse and jolted him into the dirt, his rifle on the other side of the mount. He had no pistol.

Colt charged his horse the last fifty feet and leaped off, landing on the run. When he stopped, his boot pressed hard against the man's throat.

"Who the hell are you?" Colt demanded. The man couldn't talk. Colt eased up his boot and then kicked him in the side. "Talk, damn you!"

Lieutenant Phillips raced up. He had been on the other side of the troop when the attack took place.

"I know this man, Colonel," Phillips said. "He's a trooper from G Company. Lieutenant Zennican is the troop commander."

"Christ, look at him bleed," Colt said so the man could hear. "No way to stop all that blood. I'll give him an hour, maybe, to live. We have a priest with us? Are you Catholic, boy? You got religion?"

The sniper scowled, shook his head.

"What's your name, son?"

"Corporal Farley Dennis."

"Well, Corporal Farley Dennis, not a hell of a lot we can do for you. You ever shot at a Colonel before, or is this your first try at murder?"

"Ain't talking."

"Fine. You lay there bleeding and I'll sit here watching. We could get up some bets how long you'll live."

Colt looked at Lieutenant Phillips and

winked. "How about it, Phillips? We each put in two dollars and the one who picks the closest number of minutes wins. You go see who can get in on it."

"Yeah, why not?" Phillips said and went back to the troops.

"So, I'm in for sixty minutes," Colt called. He looked at the corporal. "Sure as hell wish I hadn't shot so straight. I wanted to wound you, not kill you. But hell, we all make mistakes. Where you from, boy?"

"Arizona Territory. You really gambling about when I'm gonna die?"

"Hell yes. What else you good for? From Arizona, huh? Well, we'll bury you good and deep right here in Kansas."

"I'm not really dying. Can't be. I don't even feel much pain."

"Watched a lot of men die in the Civil War, boy. That's the way it is near the end. Numb, don't feel a thing, then suddenly, zap, and you're gone."

"You don't seem to be mad at me. That's cause I missed, I guess."

"Yeah. Then too, I can't rightly stay mad at a corpse. Sure hope they paid you well for this. It's a serious court martial offense shooting at an officer. If you wasn't dying you'd be looking at thirty years hard labor."

"Christ! They said not to miss."

Lieutenant Phillips came back and stood behind Colt watching, listening, witnessing.

"How much was I worth?"

"A hundred dollars! A whole year's pay as a corporal."

"I figured I'd be worth more. But then they don't have much money, I guess."

"Lordy, my shoulder is hurting like fire! Maybe I ain't dead yet."

"Not yet, but soon. The pain and numb comes and goes. Captain Laughton tell you to gun me?"

"Naw, don't even know him. Seen him, though. Lieutenant Zennican, my Troop Commander. He was the one. Gave me the money late last night. He'll be damned mad I told you." Dennis laughed. "What the hell, how can he hurt me now that I'm almost dead."

"Yeah, joke's on him. Any other officers involved?"

"He didn't say."

Colt took a pad of paper out of his pocket. "I'm gonna write down what you told me, and then I want you to sign it. Okay? Then I'll have something to show cause, since you won't be around to say what you told me."

"Oh, god that hurts! How much time I got left, Colonel?"

"By your color, I'd say another half hour. I seen lots of men die in the big war."

"Hell, let me sign that. I don't read too good. You read it back to me."

Colt read what the corporal had told him about being hired for a hundred dollars to murder Colonel Colt Harding.

"What the hell, might as well sign it." He took the pencil and with a lot of effort signed his name.

Lieutenant Phillips took the paper and added his name as a witness, putting down the time of day and the date. He stood.

Colt put the signed and witnessed confession in his blouse pocket and then stood. "Get up, Dennis. I just decided you ain't dying at all. You'll more than live long enough to spend those thirty years in Leavenworth prison."

"What the hell? Really? I ain't dying?" His face clouded. "You low down skunk! You tricked me."

"So sue me, you damn bushwhacker!" Colt roared. "Now get up and walk before I kick your ass all the way back to the fort!"

They marched the corporal over to the unit, leading his horse and pushing the rifle back in the army rings designed to hold it to the saddle.

"Tie him up, he'll stay with us until our training is over," Colt ordered. "Then he walks, runs, or is dragged back to the fort."

Colt insisted that the drill continue. He made the men run through it ten times. Soon some of them were up to a trot, a few could manage hanging off their saddles and firing at a gallop. Twelve of the black troopers hit the target three of the five shots to qualify and were excused from further drill on it.

They rode back to the fort with their prisoner in tow. A quarter-inch tent rope from a trooper's saddlebag served as the lead line. They only had a five mile ride. By the time they rode through the camp to the parade grounds, they had attracted fifty troopers and dependants following along.

Colt held the company in formation and sent Lieutenant Phillips to find Lieutenant Zennican and bring him to the formation.

It was a nervous five minutes before Lieutenant Zennican came striding across the parade grounds. He stopped before the mounted Lieutenant Colonel and saluted.

"First Lieutenant Zennican reporting, sir!"

Colt did not return the salute. "This man is from your troop. Is that correct?"

"Yes, sir. His name is Corporal Dennis."

"He is now Private Dennis. He is now under arrest and is to be confined to the stockade until his court martial for attempted murder, my murder.

"Every commander is responsible for every man in his unit. I'm listing you as a co-conspirator in this attack. You'll be able to explain it all before the court martial."

"Sir, I don't understand," Lieutenant Zennican said. Colt ignored the plea.

"As of right now, *Mr.* Zennican, you are released from your duties and confined to your quarters. You don't rate a salute. Lieutenant Phillips, call the Sergeant of the Guard and have this man confined."

"Yes, sir."

Lieutenant Phillips sent a sergeant to bring back the guard. Colt turned his mount and rode to the Commander's office where he handed his horse to an orderly and walked inside.

Colt's frown changed to a big grin as soon as he saw the Fort Commander.

"Damn, Colonal Roberts. We've got somebody scared shitless. They sent out

Corporal, now Private Dennis to try to bushwhack me this afternoon. He missed."

Colt told him about his confrontation with Lieutenant Bartlett the night before and about the attack on him today.

"How the hell could a corporal miss with a rifle at 300 yards?"

"He only had a target for the first shot. Then I rode off the side of the horse until I got there. That circus riding, as some call it, probably saved my life. I want to file charges. Attempted murder. I scared the shit out of his Troop Commander, too. I want him listed as a co-conspirator to attempted murder. I confined him to his quarters. I'd like you to give the official order to him and get the proceedings started.

"We may have to chisel away at this thing one or two men at a time until we get them all."

"Will that confession hold up? You have it in writing? Do you have another witness? Oh, yes, Phillips, and he signed the confession, too. Good move. I'll get the paper work started. We can leave Zennican under house arrest, and put Dennis in the paymaster's office. I had a new lock put on the door."

The Fort Commander sat back down and

shook his head. "Colt, you sure do get things stirred up once you hit an army post, don't you? You think this attack could have been a result of your threats to Bartlett last night?"

"Might be. Things are going to start fitting together here pretty soon. We're finding out more of the players, at least. Did Major Forsyth get off on his track and kill mission?"

"Yep. Left about seven this morning. He said we probably won't hear from him again. He'll hit the Republican tributaries and then swing back through Nebraska, then back into Kansas, and probably head for Ft. Hays or Ft. Riley.

"Sounded like a good man. I know Phil Sheridan keeps him around for some of his toughest assignments."

"He's got a mean one now. I hear there are more than two-thousand hostiles up in that area where he's headed. Course they aren't all in one group."

"We can't worry about that. We've got problems enough of our own right here on the post."

It was a little after two in the morning when they changed the interior guard at the old paymaster's office. The guard had been slugged, tied up and gagged. Inside, the Corporal of the Guard found the prisoner dead in his bunk, a long thin knife lay on the floor beside him.

XI

EARLY THE NEXT morning, Colt questioned the guard on the paymaster's room where the prisoner was killed. The private had no idea who had hit him from behind. He was alert, had heard nothing. Next thing he knew, he woke up tied and gagged. Colt talked with him for an hour. At the end of that time his gut feeling was that the man was telling the truth.

There would be no reason for collusion here. The killer slipped up on the man, knocked him out, broke the lock into the paymaster's office and killed Farley Dennis with the Chicago ice pick kind of long thin knife. The fact that the knife was left behind was a slap in the face, a challenge.

The killer was telling them that he had also killed Paul Winfield and they still didn't know who it was.

Colonel Roberts was boiling.

"How the hell can I run a post when all

this killing keeps going on? Now we've got an attempted murder charge against an officer and a dead witness. My suggestion is to let the charge drop. We couldn't win against an officer, not without convincing evidence. You and Phillips could have made up this story out of whole cloth and we both know the defense lawyer would play that for all it was worth. So we drop the charges. He's still a suspect in all of these killings. He and Captain Laughton."

Colt read his reports from his men watching Laughton. He hadn't got the new men to shadow the other officers yet. Laughton had done nothing out of the ordinary in the last two days. No help there. The man was in this up to his eyebrows. But how to prove it?

Colt spent an hour with Lieutenant Phillips outlining the schedule of training for the Lightning Troop. They would finish the shoot under the head tactic, then work on picking up a downed trooper at a gallop. He arranged for the Indian scouts to teach tracking and smokeless fire building and hand to hand fighting.

"I've got to get on another project, Phillips. But I'm sure you can do this. Train them hard. Weed out any men who can't stand the physical strain. Twenty rounds of target practice a day, and a two mile run every other day before morning chow. Now get out of here and get to work. Oh, Phillips, remember that all officers and sergeants take all of the training as well."

Phillips rubbed his shoulder. "So well I remember. I hit the dirt once yesterday, remember?" He grinned, waved and left.

Colt paced the porch outside the Commander's office. What the hell to do next? He had pushed Bartlett about as far as he could. Zennican would be furious to be charged, and gloating about the charges being dropped. Colt had the man right in his sights, with all the evidence he needed, and now it had been snatched away by a foul murder. Zennican was a suspect in that killing as well.

He saw the lookout come running up to the porch and hurried inside. Major Franke came out a moment later.

"We got some real troubles now," Franke said.

A wagon came toward the headquarters then. It had been a covered wagon once, but now the ribs stuck out from a burned off top, a man lay wounded on the front seat and another driving one mule was bare to the waist with blood covering his whole torso. He seemed about ready to fall over.

Half a dozen troopers ran out and helped him down. Two more wagons in much the same condition came behind this one. Colt knelt beside the driver. He was still conscious.

"Who were they?" Colt asked.

"Indians, all I know. About fifty of them hit us just before we got moving this morning. We had repeating rifles and drove the bastards off, but not before they shot flaming arrows and enough rifle rounds to almost wipe us out."

Doctor Captain Jay Judson ran across the compound with his field medical kit. He took over, directing litters be brought and two men and a woman were taken to the infirmary.

He patched up two others where they sat in the dusty shade of the wagon.

"Which way did they head?" Colt asked.

"North. We killed three of them. They killed Wilton. Still I think they come out ahead. We put down two of their ponies, but they shot six of our mules."

"Any of your people fit enough to ride out and show us where you were hit?"

"I am, sir."

Colt looked up at a boy of ten or eleven. He had sandy hair, steel blue eyes and had been crying.

"My pa was killed back there."

Colt nodded and looked for Colonel Roberts. "I want two companies to give chase, sir," Colt said.

"Two? I've got George Troop getting saddled up."

"I'd like one more, a white troop."

Colonel Roberts looked up quickly. "Think that's a good idea?"

"Yes, let's do it."

Colt ran for his quarters to get his field gear and came back five minutes later. An orderly had a horse ready for him with field gear, blanket and rations for four days.

"Three Arapaho scouts," Colt barked and another orderly rode for the Indian village just outside the post.

The troops moved out a half hour later. George Troop was commanded by Lieutenant Quint Nardo. Colt had never met the man. The second company was Captain Laughton's Baker Troop. The orders had come so fast and movement so quick that Colt didn't realize that Laughton commanded the white troopers until they were ready in the line of march.

Colt led the force with Lieutenant Nardo and the boy.

"Willy is my name, sir," he said.

"Lead the way, Willy. You know that when we find the attack site you'll be coming back to the fort?"

"Yes, sir."

Willy never wavered. He led out on a big cavalry horse and took them at a canter through two ravines, up the side of a small rise and down into a low spot beside a ribbon of water where they had camped. It was a spot only three miles from the fort.

Colt sent his three Arapahos out in advance when the boy pointed to the spot. By the time the troops reached the camp, the scouts had found the trail leading north.

Colt thanked Willy and asked him if he could find the fort.

"Yes, sir. I'm twelve. I can do that." He waved and rode off.

Colt lifted the troopers into a canter and followed the scouts who were leapfrogging each other as they did a fast track and the 95 men and officers pounded across the Kansas plains.

After an hour on the trail, Colt called back the lead scout. He spoke little English but enough to communicate.

"How many?" Colt asked.

The Arapaho held up both hands, closed them, and opened them three times.

"Thirty mounts. Are they Sioux?"

"Cheyenne," the scout said. "Raiding."

"Back trail scouts?"

"No back trail."

Colt didn't know how the scout could be so sure. They rode another two hours and were about eighteen miles from the fort. The lead scout came back and halted the troop.

He rode up to Colt. "Smoke ahead. Big Smoke."

Colt went up and took a look. It was just over a small rise near a stream. It had been a startup ranch, with a house, a barn and two corrals. Now everything was in smoking ruins. Colt used his binoculars and counted six dead horses. That wasn't like the Cheyenne to kill horses. He saw two bodies in the yard.

Colt told Lieutenant Nardo to send a detail down to check out the spot and the main body proceeded.

The report came back that all were dead, six in the family, three children, three adults.

They rode. An hour before darkness, Colt called a halt and gave the troops time to get their horses tended to and their evening meal cooked before dark. Every trooper cooked on his own on the trail. Some boiled their salt pork, mixed it with hardtack and called it supper. Some ate hardtack and boiled coffee.

Colt had the scouts out tracking until darkness stopped them. They came back.

"Cheyenne stop an hour ahead."

"They know we follow? That we here, *aqui*."

The scout shook his head.

Colt knew with a disciplined Lightning Troop he could slip up on the Cheyenne, but not the jangling, loud talking, men he now commanded.

"We'll be up at four without the bugle," Colt told the two troop commanders. "We'll be riding at five and hope to catch the bastards just at daybreak."

It didn't work out that way. The Cheyenne had left during the night. They had someone on their back trail after all.

For six hours Colt chased the Cheyenne, then surprisingly, the band turned to fight. They had selected a small valley with a dry stream bed. The land rose fifty feet to the flatness of the plains. Colt brought up his troops when the Scouts reported the Cheyenne had stopped.

Captain Laughton had been quiet during the ride, had kept with his men and reported only when ordered to. He was still angry and Colt wasn't sure why.

"I'll lead George Troop on the attack," Colt said. "Captain Laughton, you hold in reserve and out of sight back here. If you see any movement from the side, any new Indian forces, or hear the attack call on the bugle, you move in at once. Is that clear?"

Captain Laughton nodded and Colt returned to Lieutenant Nardo.

"Here's your chance to earn your pay, Lieutenant. We're leading the attack so let's get in motion. Put your men with Spencer repeaters in the first ranks. Let's go!"

The bugler sounded the attack call and George Troop moved out in two long ranks across the narrow valley.

"Hold your fire until I give the command to fire!" Colt bellowed over the sound of hooves on the rich soil.

Fifty yards from the red men he fired his Spencer and the other weapons spoke. The Indians split into two groups, half raced off toward a fork in the small creek and its valley and the rest circled to the left.

Before he could stop them, half of the troops charged away after the supposedly retreating Cheyenne. Colt knew what was happening. A trap! Was it too late to stop the dividing tactic? He called to the bugler to sound the attack call, the signal for Laughton to bring in his troop.

Laughton's forces never moved.

Colt saw the trap sprung as more than a hundred wildly screaming red men charged out of the low ridges and hit the Negro troopers from the side. He ordered the bugler to sound retreat and slowly the blue uniformed troopers worked their way to the rear where they could regroup before the larger force of Indians could attack again.

That was all that saved them. The plains Indians were notorious for their lack of discipline in battle. The war chiefs were advisors only, and each man and group of braves did about what he wanted to in the heat of battle.

Now it gave Colt time to have the bugler sound the assembly call and send a messenger to Laughton. At last, Laughton raced up with his fifty men from behind the cover they had been in and into the small valley to reinforce the black troops.

When the Cheyenne saw the fresh troops,

they hesitated. A dozen warriors turned away and rode north. A few stragglers followed. Then the war chief lifted his war lance and the rest of the raiders turned and rode away, leaving only a rear guard of a dozen braves to watch the bluecoats a quarter-of-a-mile away.

"Casualty report!" Colt thundered and the black sergeants picked it up and began counting their men.

Colt looked at the bugler. "Where's Lieutenant Nardo?"

The private shook his head. "Last I saw of him he went after the group to the left up the small ravine."

Colt took six men and charged up the ravine. They found four dead troopers around the expired Lieutenant. All had been hacked with war axes and split open with knives. It was an old superstition most plains Indians held. To mutilate a corpse in this life, meant the man's spirit would be cut and torn in the next life and not be a strong adversary.

They caught the horses, put the dead troopers over them and rode back to the main body.

Colt rode directly to Captain Laughton. He was so angry his face had flushed and his back was ramrod stiff. He reined in beside the Captain.

"Where the hall were you when I signalled for you to join the fight?" Colt asked coldly.

Laughton shrugged. "I heard no call to attack. The first I knew you wanted us was when your messenger arrived."

"Liar!" Colt exploded. He slammed his mount into the Captain's, almost unseating him. "Every man in your command heard the call. You'll be up on charges of insubordination, and failure to follow a direct order just as soon as we hit the fort. You are hereby relieved of your command. I'll take your weapons, now!"

Laughton shrugged, handed over his pistol and his rifle.

"No court martial at Ft. Wallace gonna convict me of not charging into a fight just to save the asses of some jig-a-boos, Colonel. You're way out of line."

Colt had to fight with himself to keep from knocking the smirking man out of his saddle.

"Mister Laughton, you'll ride at the end of the company. Sergeant, take command of your company and prepare to move out."

"Yes, sir," the three striper said.

Back with the Negro troops, Colt took the casualty report. Seven men had been killed and twelve wounded. One man could ride, but shouldn't.

His sergeant rode up and shook his head.

"Johnson, sir, he can't live more than an hour. Could we put off the march until then?"

Colt ordered the men to form up in march order, then to dismount. The men patched themselves up the best they could. Some day the army would send some kind of medical people into the field with the troops. Not doctors, but someone with enough training to bind up wounds and stop bleeding and save lives. Someday.

An hour and a half later, Johnson died. They rode.

It was just past dark when they trailed into Ft. Walker and Colt dismissed the troops. Now his real work was just beginning. He had more charges to file, he had to see how he could pressure Lieutenant Bartlett again. Somehow this all had to wrap up with the discovery of the identity of the Brotherhood and its breakup. But right now he had no idea how that would happen.

XII

LIEUTENANT LEROY ROBERTS sat in his Infantry Company C office when Lieutenant Ivan Bartlett stormed in, his face frozen in anger. His voice was low but boiling with emotions barely controlled.

"You did it, didn't you, you insignificant worm? You ran to daddy and told him everything and he told Colonel Harding. What do you think we are, stupid?"

Leroy Roberts jumped to his feet. A sudden anger washing over him.

"I did not tell anyone about that night. Nothing! I gave you my word as an officer! You apologize this minute or you'll be sorry!"

"You're going to fight with me? Good."

Both men had been through West Point. There, both had to undergo strenuous physical combat. Roberts lashed out with a right fist so quickly that the smaller man couldn't defend against it. The blow struck solidly and Bartlett's head rocked back, his eyes closed and he sighed as he fall against the wall and slid to the floor. He was unconscious.

Lieutenant Roberts snorted. The little man had a glass jaw—a big mouth and a glass jaw. His right punch was still a good one. At one point he'd tried out for the Point's boxing team, but decided to concentrate on his studies.

Roberts knelt and slapped Bartlett's face gently.

"Come on, Bartlett, wake up. This is no place for a nap. Snap out of it, Bartlett. Bartlett!" Roberts shouted his name directly into his ear and that brought him around.

"My god, who hit me?" He blinked and looked up. "You? You knocked me out with one punch? I don't believe it."

"Stand up and I'll show you exactly how I did it. You can do that right after you apologize for calling me a liar."

Roberts stood in front of the man who still sat on the floor. Roberts's fists were tight and ready as he scowled at the other officer.

"I'll say it once more. I did not tell anyone about the other night. If someone else knows, one of the other men said something, or someone saw it happen. Maybe the black man told his sergeant."

"Not a chance. He's afraid of being dead."

Bartlett struggled to stand up and rubbed his jaw. "I don't understand you, Roberts."

"Who does? I don't understand myself. But you better believe that I didn't tell anyone about the other night. If it got out, if Colonel Harding knows about it, he didn't find out from me."

"He said something about . . ." Bartlett stopped. "Never mind."

He threw up his hands. "Okay, I believe you. Just keep your trap shut about it." He turned and went out the door and closed it harder than was necessary.

For a short minute, Leroy Roberts smiled. Then he thought about his afternoon appointment. He had done it, talked to the woman who cleaned up his room and did his laundry. She was the wife of a corporal and everyone knew she was strictly an officers' woman.

He put on his command face and walked out. "I'll be out the rest of the afternoon, corporal. Take any orders I have coming in and hold them."

Well done, he told himself silently. He

even sounded like a U.S. Army First Lieutenant.

He was a few minutes early when he entered his quarters. He didn't care who saw him, they were his rooms. He wasn't sure what to do, so he picked up a book and started reading. He was momentarily startled when someone rattled his door, then came in.

Tessie carried a mop bocket, a mop and another bucket with her various cleaning things in them. She put them down and smiled at him.

"Well, looks like this is the day, eh, Lieutenant."

She caught his hand and led him into the small bedroom. She looked around, then reached up and kissed him. She put one of his hands over her breasts and hugged him. When he made no further move, she unbuttoned the blouse she wore and swung it open.

He stared at her breasts. So big and so heavy and such large nipples! For just a moment he thought of that girl back in school, then he touched her breasts and he felt the hot blood at his crotch. He gave a little yelp of delight and pushed her gently down on the bed.

A half hour later he sat up and wanted to cry. He never even had attained an erection.

"Still no luck," Tessie said. She hung her big breasts near his face but he pushed her away.

"Forget it, Tessie. Your two dollars are on the dresser anyway. You did your part. Just not my day. Next time."

He couldn't wait until she dressed and left. Then he fell on the bed and wept. Tears rolled down his cheeks and soaked into the quilt. He trembled. What the hell was the matter with him?

He didn't make it to mess that evening. Instead he sat and stared into the small fire he built in his fireplace. It was far from cold, but he enjoyed a small blaze.

Again he thought of the girl in the woods near his home and he marveled how easy it had been. Today had been a disaster. So she wasn't pretty or thin, she was a woman.

Just after seven, a messenger came with a note that he should report to the Commander's office.

He dressed, shined his shoes, brushed his hair and walked up to see his father.

He had decided that he would not tell him about the abortive try at infiltrating the Brotherhood. He couldn't do the job. That was plain to him. He'd beg off the assignment, somehow.

Colonel Roberts had just finished a mixed drink of whiskey and branch water, and he was relaxing.

"Things going to hell around here, you know that? Your old man is about to get his ass racked. You done anything to help?"

"No, sir. I can't. I tried and it didn't work. You'll have to get someone else to get into the Brotherhood."

"Can't. Want a drink? A real man's drink, whiskey and branch water?"

Leroy nodded, took the drink and sipped it. He relaxed. He was off the spit on the Brotherhood thing.

"Hell, it's too far along to try to get inside. Now any new man would be under suspicion. Wanted to tell you not to worry about it. If Colt Harding can't solve the puzzle, I'll go ahead and take some desk job in supply. Yeah, that would suit my talents as a field officer. In the goddamn supply depot in Washington or in Omaha. Shit, I'd die of boredom in a month."

He pulled at a new drink.

Colonel Roberts looked at his son. "You're not talking much tonight."

"Not much to say." He sipped the drink.

Should he tell his father he tried to fuck a woman this afternoon and couldn't even get it up? Should he tell him he still pounded off on his bed when he thought of that naked fifteen year old girl back home? For a moment it was almost funny. But he couldn't laugh. His whole life was one sad joke.

He stood. "I can't get drunk. I'm Officer of the Guard tomorrow."

"Goddamn yes. Duty first. Here I am looking at the end of my army career and you're too damned proud to drink with me."

Leroy sat back down and poured another drink. He couldn't even feel the whiskey. He drank it down and watched his father getting drunker and drunker. In an hour he'd have to walk him to his quarters or he'd never make it.

It only took a half hour.

When Leroy came out of the Fort Commander's quarters he turned at once toward his own digs. Two men fell in step beside him. One was Lieutenant Ivan Bartlett. The other, Lieutenant Zennican. Well away from the colonel's quarters they stopped in the darkness.

Zennican grabbed Leroy's shirt front and twisted. He was half a head taller than Lieutenant Roberts.

"So you didn't run to daddy, did you? What were you just doing, figuring out the fort budget?"

"I was helping my father get drunk. I accomplished my mission and now I'm on my way to my quarters."

"Think you'll get there?"

Zennican let go of his shirt and slapped him hard across the face. Roberts pawed for the .44 caliber Colt at his side. Zennican punched him in the belly and he doubled over in pain. The big officer's ironlike hand jolted upward into Roberts's chin and he sprawled on his back in the dust.

"I think you talked to daddy, little boy. When I find out for damned sure, you're a dead daddy's boy. You hear that, Roberts? When I know for damn sure, you're ready for the worms."

Zennican kicked him in the side, then the two officers faded into the darkness.

Leroy Roberts struggled to sit up. He was still dizzy. The booze and the beating meshed together to keep him unable to walk for five minutes. Then his head cleared and he made it to his quarters.

He sagged on the bed.

What was the use? He was a failure at everything he tried. Women, the army, helping his father. His company was not even the best at the fort. He took out his revolver and stared at it. He was a dead man. Zennican had said so.

Leroy fell on the bed and let the tears come. He was good at crying. Shit, he could do that easy. For the flash of a moment he thought of the bare male bodies in the shower at West Point. He'd worked through that. But now he called it up, thought back. Dozens of times he'd had a rock hard-on when he came out of the showers, hiding it with his towel.

Was he really a homosexual? There was one way to find out. But he was never going to find out for sure. Knowing for sure hung over his neck like a saber poised, ready to be swung down with killing force.

One way or another, what did it matter?

He picked up the revolver again and checked the loads, five, riding on the empty cylinder. He pushed the barrel in his mouth and eased his finger onto the trigger.

A metal taste, slightly oily. It tasted blue. Somehow it seemed so right, so natural.

That was crazy. Oh, sure, let Zennican dismember him, let Zennican cut his balls off and stuff them down his throat!

"Betsy," he said the name out loud. That

was the girl's name back home, that glorious afternoon in the woods when they both were naked and learning about each other, and touching and feeling and becoming excited and stopping just short of intercourse, but doing everything else.

He thought about Betsy. He wished she were here. He kept thinking about undressing Betsy and soon stretched out on the bed. He remembered the last time when she had slipped him into her mouth and he had ejaculated at once and she coughed and then smiled and then took him again.

As he remembered his hips bucked against the army blanket and he cried. As he sobbed he took the Colt and put the muzzle in his mouth, pushed it far back and up high.

Then he pulled the trigger quickly before he could change his mind.

Colt Harding heard the shot and got there before anyone else. His quarters were just two doors down. He did what he could, but there wasn't much. He covered the naked body with a blanket. The revolver had frozen inside the soldier's mouth. His arm had set as in a vice.

There was little left of the top of Lieutenant Roberts's head. The big .44 slug had expanded and taken off most of his skull splattering it around the bedroom.

Colt closed the bedroom door and sent the curious away from the door. Then he went to find Colonel Roberts.

The Post Commander was in bed. His wife answered the door explaining that her husband had been drinking. She couldn't wake him now if she wanted to.

Another six hours wouldn't hurt a thing. Colt went back to Lieutenant Roberts's quarters and called the Corporal of the Guard. He ordered a guard set on the door. No one was to enter the door before Colonel Colt Harding came back. No one.

Colt had a hard time getting to sleep that night. The kid was twenty-four, maybe twenty-five. He had his whole life ahead of him, a West Pointer, a future in the army. Now, with a quick trigger pull—eternity.

He was up at five and knocked on the Colonel's door at six. Colonel Roberts came himself, bleary eyed and hoarse.

"Sir, I have some bad news for you. Could we sit down somewhere?" They sat at the kitchen table.

"One of your men has shot himself, sir. He's dead."

"Christ, what else is going to happen

here?" He stood and walked to the door, then came back and sat down.

"Okay, who was it?"

"Your son."

For a moment, Colonel Darrell Roberts stared at Colt. Then slowly his face broke into small pieces of agony and he began to sob and lowered his face into his hands on the top of the table. He cried for five minutes.

When he could speak, he shook his head. "I pushed him too hard. I made him try to get into the Brotherhood. I don't know how close he got. He told me he couldn't do it. Kid had guts to tell his old man that. I said I was about to get booted into retirement. I pushed him too hard."

"Be better if you don't see him the way he is," Colt said.

Colonel Roberts shook his head. "No. My job. My fault. I'll get my good shirt on. You told anyone else?"

"No."

"Go get Doctor Judson. Then meet me there. I want some time with him first, alone."

"He's in the bedroom."

Colt left quickly. That was the hardest job he'd ever had to do, anytime, anywhere.

XIII

THE BUSINESS OF Ft. Wallace moved along at what looked like its normal pace, but the whole place was slowed down and shocked at the death. The jolt of a suicide among the officer corps is taken much harder by those officers than when one of their group was accidentally killed.

Colt couldn't question Colonel Roberts about his son, but it seemed fairly certain that it had been a suicide. Colt had to break down the door when he arrived at Lieutenant Robert's quarters last night. It had been solidly locked from the inside and the windows nailed shut, as they all were, to help keep out the Kansas winter cold.

It was a feeling he had more than anything, but Colt decided this death had been suicide. As the fort settled back into the normal routine, Colt tried to go over all the odds and ends he had to put together here at Ft. Wallace on his assignment.

There were the two deaths of officers,

both of a suspicious nature, and probably engineered by the Brotherhood.

He had a small victory with Steve Sapp, the private who had covered up the dumping of the body. That produced two officer names. He had pressured Lieutenant Bartlett and had had some partial success.

It was possible that the attempt on his life the following day after that pressure on Lieutenant Bartlett, had been a direct result of hassling the officer. Which left Lieutenant Zennican, a brutal, mean kind of officer who probably was not from the Point. He and Bartlett had moved Lieutenant Winfield's body into the paddock.

So they must know who killed him. Zennican, or Bartlett, or maybe Captain Laughton. The Captain had failed to attack on orders in the last engagement. It could have been a deliberate attempt to allow the Indians to kill more of the Negro troops and Colt at the same time. He still had to deal with Laughton on the failure to obey court martial.

It also looked like Laughton was the main spring in the Brotherhood. He was the highest rank in the group. Damn! He had some of the pieces but nothing fit. Nothing meshed together to form a complete picture.

Maybe the three men watching Laughton would turn up something else. Maybe.

Lieutenant Colonel Colt Harding asked the orderly to bring around his horse, and he charged away from the fort to the west where he knew the Lightning Troop would be in training about a mile away along the Smoky Hill River. It was nearly dry now this late in the year.

Colt heard the troops five minutes before he saw them. He came along a small side draw, ground tied his army mount and slipped up toward the men who were trying the pickup maneuver with their horses moving at a walk. Every other man hit the dirt. Once both men fell off the horse. The troopers shouted and screamed with glee.

Colt lay looking at the troop through a screen of dry weeds. He drew his revolver and put five shots over the men's heads. They dove for cover.

Colt jumped up and bellowed at them.

"What the hell you think this is, a Sunday School picnic? Lieutenant Phillips, front and center!"

Phillips rode up and saluted.

"Sir—"

"Save it!" Colt snapped. "I don't ever want to see this troop in the field without some security out. I want one man on each of the four sides, alert and watching outward. Is that clear, mister?"

"Yes, sir."

"Post your security. Dismounted and out of sight. Whenever you're away from the fort, consider yourself in a hostile situation. The savages could attack you at any time. They are around here this close sometimes. Remember those wagons? Set out your men."

"Yes, sir!"

Colt grinned. The kid was going to be all right. He caught his horse's reins and walked down to the exercise area. The men had missed one key hand hold position to vault into the saddle. He demonstrated with one of the larger men.

"Hit the saddle here, grab, bounce if you need to, and then swing up on the back of the horse. Rider, look for the best spot to grab the man coming up. It might be his hand, his arm, even the back of his shirt. Drag him on board. Now, do it again. We're going to be here until every man has made one pickup, and has been picked up."

They were there until nearly dark. All but one man, the oldest man in the troop, had passed the test.

By the time they rode back to the post it was full dark. The company clerks would prepare chow, as they always did, so the men would not miss the meal.

Colt did miss the officers' mess, but one of the cooks saw him come in and brought over a tray for him to his quarters. It was probably better food than the other officers had been served. But rank had a few privileges.

After Colt ate, the cook picked up the tray and dishware. Colt thanked him and the man seemed surprised. He wasn't used to being treated with dignity.

Colt had his orderly take a message to Lieutenant Bartlett. It was time they had another small talk. Bartlett came in and was surprised when Colt offered him a shot of whiskey straight from the bottle. He accepted.

"Bartlett, I'm disappointed in you," Colt began. "The last time we talked I suggested that you had been one of the men who beat up those two Negro troopers. Then what should happen the very next day, but that Corporal Dennis is paid a hundred dollars to take a shot at me."

"I heard about that, sir."

"I bet you did. I can't prove it, but I'd

make a bet that you were one of the men who raised the hundred dollars for Dennis. He never did get to spend that money, did he?"

Bartlett set the shot glass down on the table.

"You have no right to accuse me of illegal acts, Colonel, unless you are bringing charges."

"Charges? What the hell you talking about? I invite you over for a friendly drink. So we talk a little." He filled the shot glass again and his own, then lifted his. "Not polite not to drink with the host, Barlett. Bottoms to the ceiling!" Colt drained his. Bartlett hesitated, then did the same.

They both sat at the small kitchen table.

"What the hell I can't figure out is this damn Brotherhood. Oh, yeah, we know most everything about it. You're a member, so is Zennican and so is that damned Captain Laughton who tried to get me killed. He's still up on charges. Wonder if the paperwork is through on that yet? Fucker tried to let the Cheyenne or Sioux, or whoever they were, lift my scalp.

"He pushed it too far and now I'm gonna lift his shoulder boards and his captain's rank."

Colt belched, laughed and poured another shot for them. He sipped at it.

"Bartlett, don't feel sorry for Laughton. You're the boy who's in the most trouble. I got a witness who puts you at the beating of the Negroes. I got another witness who will swear in a court martial that you and Lieutenant Zennican carried Lieutenant Winfield's body into the paddock and then worked twenty minutes to drive the horses over his body. You are in one hell of a lot of trouble, little man."

Bartlett snapped his head around to watch Colt as he finished the accusation. His hand trembled as he reached for his shot glass. "Just who is your witness, Colonal?"

Colt began to put on some signs of being drunk. He leaned in the chair, almost spilled the drink as he reached for it. A few of his words were slurred now as he put on an act for the younger man.

"Hey, hey. Don't try and get facts out of me before the trial. Your lawyer will know all about it soon enough." He belched again and apologized.

"What the hell, maybe we can get you off, after all." He stared drunkenly at Bartlett. "Shit for breakfast, Lieutenant, just because you carried in the body, don't mean you pushed the knife into him, or mashed his head with a pistol butt. Christ no. You coulda." Colt looked at him, squinting his eyes. "But I don't think you knifed him. Oh, you was there. I figure that. Also guess that when the axe of that court martial comes down toward your neck, you'll be glad to tell us exactly who killed the two officers and Corporal Dennis."

Colt stared at him. "Yep, way we figure it is that you'll be more than glad, anxious in fact, to lay it all out for us and then you won't be charged with nothing." Colt lifted his glass and drained it. When he put it down on the table the small glass tipped over.

Lieutenant Bartlett watched him. "Sir, is there anything else we should talk about?"

Colt righted the glass, then with a steady hand balanced it on top of the whiskey bottle, then balanced Bartlett's glass on top of that. His hand was steel steady, his eye clear and angry.

"Bartlett," he said in a calm, steady undrunk voice, "when we talked before it was a simple matter of beating up two men. Now what we're discussing is murder, the cold blooded killing of three men, Lieutenant Wilson, Lieutenant Winfield and Corporal Dennis.

"Any one of these is a hanging affair and you damn well better start thinking about that. We know all about the Brotherhood. We know where you meet, when you meet, how many attend, and we're quickly putting together a complete list of the ten or eleven officers who attend.

"Your bare ass is hanging out, mister. You're about ready to sit on a red hot grill with no pants to protect you. The only way you can save your bare ass is to cooperate fully with me . . . and do it right now. You understand your position?"

"Not entirely, sir." Bartlett picked his glass off the top of the stack and drained it. "Say it out plain to me, Colonel."

"One, you'll be charged with conspiracy to murder Lieutenant Winfield. Two, you'll be charged with moving the body and another conspiracy to cover up the crime. Three, you'll be charged with withholding information of a criminal act . . . murder by person or persons unknown. Four, you'll be charged with the assault and beating of the two Negro men.

"As we move into the court martial, I'm sure we'll uncover other charges against you.

You'll be convicted on all counts and get from seventy five to a hundred and twenty years in prison. How does that fit in with your promotion schedule to Captain?"

Bartlett's sly grin from moments before when he thought the colonel was drunk had evaporated in a second. Sweat glistened on his forehead in the kerosene lamplight. He poured himself another drink and took it in one gulp.

"Sir, you've got to believe me. I never killed any of those men. I just didn't do it."

"But you were there!"

"Well, yes, but I'm not certain who actually . . ."

"Don't lie to me, Bartlett! We've got the start of something going here that just might save your worthless hide!"

Bartlett stood and walked to the fireplace and then back. He rubbed his face with his hand, then looked at Colt.

"You give me a signed guarantee that you won't prosecute me for anything, and I'll cooperate. I've got to have that legal paper, and your promise as an officer and a gentleman that in exchange for my testimony at the court martial, any and all possible charges against me in connection with this entire Brotherhood matter will be ignored and no charges brought."

Colt held out his hand. "Agreed. I'll write up the paper tonight and expect you here tomorrow morning at ten to sign it."

Bartlett moved toward the door.

"Lieutenant, don't tell anyone about this. I'd really hate to have a fourth killing to solve—yours."

Bartlett almost missed his head with his hat as he jammed it on and hurried out the door.

Colt turned up the lamp, took out a fresh sheet of lined paper and began writing out an agreement with Lieutenant Bartlett not to prosecute him in the Brotherhood affair. Damn! He might be close to learning the truth about the three deaths. Might be. A lot could happen between now and tomorrow morning and even after he signed the agreement.

Colt wrote two drafts of the agreement, then satisfied with it he made a copy and put both in a long white envelope. He would have Lieutenant Bartlett sign both copies, give one to the Fort Commander and keep one.

Then he could start getting the information, launching the charges, and cleaning up this mess.

Colt drummed his fingers on the tabletop. He wished he could have quizzed Bartlett tonight, to find out for sure who had wielded the knife and the polo mallet which must have killed Lieutenant Wilson.

Tomorrow. He hoped for tomorrow.

Colt wrote a letter to his wife Doris back at Ft. Leavenworth. It had been a lonely time for both of them. Soon he would be home to see her and the kids. Soon. The more he thought about the Brotherhood, the better he felt. It would take just one defector, just one officer to testify against the others and it would all be over.

He was sure that Bartlett was the man. He had him right by the balls and the little man knew it. All he could do now was squirm and complain and stall. Colt wouldn't put up with any of that kind of action. He'd be more than willing to let Bartlett walk away free and unbesmirched, to get Laughton and the others. The killers were the ones he wanted most!

XIV

MAJOR GEORGE FORSYTH looked at the tracks his scout pointed to in the rich Kansas soil. They had veered north from the now dry stream bed of the Smoky River and found Beaver Creek. There were many signs of Indians. They had found and examined two abandoned camps.

There seemed to be a large group of Indians from the horse droppings and the way the available forage had been cropped low. His scouts said at least a hundred and fifty warriors and all of their traveling gear.

There were many women along, which meant it was to be, or had already been, a long campaign and the women were needed for cooking.

Forsyth checked the tracks again. They were heading to the west more. Soon they would be out of Kansas and into Colorado. The south fork of the Republican River should be ahead and then farther north the Arikara branch of the Republican which began in Colorado, worked through the far northwestern corner of Kansas, and into Nebraska before it joined the other tributaries that made up the Republican.

Somewhere in here he was going to run these bastards to ground and fight them. His troops were ready. They were rested from the two days at Ft. Wallace. Now, after seven days of working the Kansas countryside up and back, down and forward, they had at last cut a good trail.

Not even the scouts knew how many warriors there might be, but the braves were not running. Neither were they raiding here since there were no settlers. Perhaps they were scouting the land for new raids later. Soon they should be returning to their hunting camps. Major Forsyth was sure the Indian parfleches were not filled yet with all the pemmican they would need for the coming winter.

He held his hand high in the air, saw the signal repeated behind him. When his hand came down, the column of fours moved out on the trail the scouts had indicated.

More north, more west. Hell, the hostiles couldn't be much ahead of them along this trail. When the advance scouts found the main body of hostiles, it would be a good fight. Major Forsyth and his men had been ready for a fight like this for weeks.

Major Forsyth settled into his saddle. The McClellan was used by most troopers now. They didn't sit any better than they ever had. He longed for the Hope saddle he had used during the war. But that was impossible now. Maybe later.

At least the McClellan had two saddlebags, crupper, surcingle and carbine slot to hold a weapon. It would do. He sent his scouts out to try for some rabbits for the meal tonight. If they got enough with their pistols, the whole troop would eat. Otherwise he and the sergeants would have meat.

The fact he would eat better than his men didn't bother Major Forsyth. That was the army way, the officers had privileges. It would always be so in every army.

The scouts came back. They had just contacted the lead scout who said the trail continued and they would not find the hostiles' camp before nightfall.

Major George Forsyth groaned. He had wanted this to be a day of action. The major checked his pocket watch. The spring was getting weak. If he didn't remember to wind it twice a day he had to check with his top sergeant to set the timepiece. It was slightly before four P.M.

He decided that they would call a halt in the next suitable spot which had enough water for the horses. He passed the word and the scouts went at once to find a campsite.

Maybe tomorrow, Forsyth thought to himself. He needed a good engagement with the hostiles after all of this time to satisfy the men, and to justify himself with General Sheridan.

Lieutenant Colonel Colt Harding worked with the Lightning Troop the next morning. He had returned to the fort at ten when Lieutenant Bartlett came in. The small officer read the paper, then signed both and gave them back to Colt.

"I have to get back to my company right away. Two of the other officers were watching me. Someone saw me come in here last night. I don't have to tell you that if they get suspicious, I won't be able to tell you a thing until people are under arrest and in the stockade. Then I'd feel safe."

"We had an agreement. You just signed it. You'll have to talk when we are ready."

"If you want a live witness, you'll have to

go slow. I won't help your case any stretched out in a grave six feet underground, will I?"

He walked out without being excused.

Colt threw his gloves against the door as Bartlett left. Now what the hell was the matter with him? More important, was he backing out of the agreement?

Colt stormed out of his quarters and rode hard back to the training site, about a mile north of the fort. He was angry at Bartlett, at himself, at the whole damn world. Most of his fury had been worked off by the time he got to the Pony Soldiers. They were working on tracking, with the Arapahos going out as the wanted man, and a team of two troopers and one Indian tracking him.

The scout was there only to help train the men on how to find the trail, how to follow it, what to look for, and to steer them right when they went wrong.

Twice Colt took a pair of troopers out and ambushed the trackers by firing well over their heads.

"Remember when you're out this way, you're always in danger. The tougher the trail, the harder you better look for an attack. The ones you're tracking could have circled back and be waiting for you."

Training, training. Sometimes Colt

thought he was a damned school teacher. This was going to be the last Lightning Troop he set up. They could train their own from now on.

He worked with the troop until well past midday. Then he called a halt and let the men eat their rations. After the food they went to firing practice off hand, standing. It's the toughest way to fire, but Pony Soldiers often were called to shoot that way.

The targets developed few holes that afternoon.

On the way back to the fort, Lieutenant Phillips pulled up beside Colt.

"Sir, I think the men are coming along fine. They are the best marksmen of any troop I've ever worked with. They can move fast and quietly, and know how to fight when they find a band of hostiles."

"Good," Colt said. "The next emergency we get is yours. Then we'll see how good the training actually was."

"Yes, sir!" They rode in silence for a while. "Sir, the older private I had, I've arranged to transfer him to Easy Troop, and the Troop Commander there is sending me three new men to fill out my roster."

"Good. See that they are caught up in their training. First order is riding, then firing mounted and under neck and prone. Then tracking and knife fighting."

"Yes, sir."

They rode into the fort and to the parade ground.

Lieutenant Phillips asked the question that had been nagging at him. "Sir, you said the next emergency. Are we expecting some trouble?"

"Out here, Lieutenant, you have to expect trouble at any time, be ready for it. Then you have a better chance to live through it."

"Yes, sir."

"Dismiss the troops, Lieutenant," Colt said and rode over to his quarters.

He went from there straight to the Fort Commander's sergeant who handed him the envelope. Inside, the fine hand detailed the comings and goings of Captain Laughton. It had been determined that the Captain now had sexual maneuvers with his wife every Tuesday evening. Colt grinned.

Last night had been Wednesday. The report continued:

Captain Laughton's weekly poker party was held. Attending were Lieutenants Bartlett and Zennican, and Captain Oberholtzer. All arrived about seven and seemed to play cards until sometime after midnight. Near or before that time, several men slipped singly into the rear door of the Laughton quarters.

They moved to the small shed, and then worked through the shadows to the rear door and into a darkened room.

The blinds were pulled before, and what took place inside could not be determined

All of the men left about one o'clock. The same three men who had entered by the front door (poker players) left that way at about the same time.

There was no other action at the residence until morning. End of report.

Another name of a member of the Brotherhood, Captain Oberholtzer.

Major Franke came out of his office and stopped in front of Colt. "I need some more facts on the statement of charges against Captain Laughton, Colonel. Do you have time?"

Colt went with the Fort Adjutant into his office and worked for an hour to get the wording down on the charges. The papers were almost ready. They would be served on Captain Laughton, a date set for his court martial, and an officer named to serve as the Captain's defense counsel.

Colt had been through it too many times.

But this was one court martial that he would be totally involved with. The only thing that might stop it would be wrapping up the Brotherhood mess sooner than the date of the trial. That would be a highly practical way to take care of two cases at once.

Captain Laughton sat in his private office in his G Troop headquarters and slammed a riding crop against the side of his leg.

"Damnit to hell Zennican, what the fuck we going to do? We can't just sit here and let that bastard keep building up evidence against us. Got to be something."

"The first move we made against him backfired, you might say," Zennican rasped. "That one got everybody in more trouble than ever. The next plan we use has got to be worked out carefully, and then carried out by us, not some stupid enlisted."

"Fine, fine. But what the hell is our plan?"

"I'm working on it."

"You been working on it for three days now, damnit!"

"That's what we can't do, Victor. We can't lose our nerve, or we'll all wind up stretching a rope or decorating a firing squad pole. I ain't seen too many wonderful ideas coming out of your head."

The men stared at each other.

"First thing we do is stop having the meetings. We just pull back and lay low for a while."

"Then things will get bad again," Zennican said. "The Nigras will be walking all over us whites."

"Got to risk it. Somehow Harding's got some witnesses. The bastard knows too much. Could be he's twisted Steve Sapp's balls somehow and made him talk. Or Oberholtzer. Never seen a man so worried about losing his rank as Oberholtzer is."

"We ain't getting nowhere, Victor. What the hell we gonna do about Colonel Harding?"

"Shoot the bastard."

"Yeah, no argument. But how and where and who? What do we set up for alibis? Who is going to do the job? We got to have a fucking plan!"

"We do it at the next training session he has out in the prairie with his black ass troopers. You're good with a rifle, Zennican. You do the job. He'll be out tomorrow again. He rides out every day. No problem finding him on that horse of his. Only two white faces out there."

"You could set up a meeting that I'm on for some damn reason. You still Quartermaster, too?"

"Yeah. Inventory time. Report time. I could have you so deep inside the supply warehouse nobody would see you. You slip out, get a horse we'll leave close by, and you can get out to that place north of the fort where they go for training."

"They have security out?"

"When they're training? Hell no. Don't chicken out on me, Zennican. You ride up to a quarter of a mile. Get off and slip up to a hundred yards. Blast him four times with a carbine. I've got a 'Sixty Three Sharps carbine that shoots straight as a string."

"That single shot? When I do it I'll take a Spencer carbine and a Blakeslee Quickloader. I want to be able to spit out lots of rounds if I need to. Idea is to hit him so fast he won't have a chance to react. Then I get away before the damned Negroes get organized."

"Sounds good," Laughton said.

Zennican snorted. "Hell yes, you ain't gonna put your ass on the line to save the day. Shit, maybe I shouldn't either."

"You don't and we got to figure out something else, like a knife between the ribs late some dark night when he's in his bunk."

"The man is not stupid. He'll have his door double locked and a chair against it and his pistol in his right hand," Zennican said. "No chance we could get anywhere near him."

"Then it's the training area. You better make it tomorrow morning. I'll be sure and cover for you in the supply warehouse. Good luck."

"Hell, I'll need all I can get. You sure he's going out there tomorrow?"

"Goes every day. You can watch them leave, then slip away."

"I get myself killed out there, Laughton, I'm gonna haunt you every day of the rest of your life."

XV

MAJOR GEORGE FORSYTH looked at the trail they had been following. Their head scout, a corporal from Massachusetts, pointed out the travois marks, and the hundreds of horses.

"A damn lot of them hostiles on the move, sir. Must be three or four villages, at least."

"So that means they have women and children. They have to move slower. They must be back from a raid and moving to winter quarters."

"Sir, with your permission, could I make a suggestion?"

Forsyth nodded.

"I been out here a damn long time, sir. I'd say this bunch is just too big for us to handle. I'd figure maybe we should look for a smaller band."

Forsyth snorted. "Corporal, you enlisted to fight Indians, didn't you? You might never have a better chance. We move ahead as planned until we find the bastards!"

They continued that afternoon and the next day. They had crossed the south fork of the Republican River and were well toward the Arikara River. There would be little water in it this time of year, but still plenty for a band of camping Sioux, even if was made up of three or four normal sized villages.

It was a little after four in the afternoon on September 16, 1868 when Major Forsyth and his 50 hand picked troopers came through a ravine into the valley of the

Arikara River. It was a tributary to the Republican and just inside the Colorado Territory border.

He watched the flood plain for a moment then pulled up the troop and studied it well. The scout indicated that the broad trail they were following continued through the valley and upstream to the southwest.

The river itself here had a spread of 140 yards, but was mostly dry this time of the year. Upstream a short distance, he saw where the stream parted to leave a small island about 60 yards long and 20 yards wide. It was wooded with scrub alder, wild plum and willow and one single, stately cottonwood.

They had put in a good day and now that they had reached the Arikara, Forsyth called a halt. The men would have time for a rest and to feed and water their horses. Already the fifteen pounds of oats each mount carried was starting to dwindle. But there was plenty of graze here.

They made camp in a few trees near the river and put out minimum security. They had seen no back trail scouts from the Sioux. The men had a leisurely time making camp, feeding their mounts and watering them, then making their own meal.

Each of the troopers carried his own rations and did his cooking in the field. He had come with 12 days rations and already they were running low. They also carried one blanket, a canteen, a Spencer repeating rifle with 140 rounds of ammunition, and a ten tube Blakeslee Quickloader.

The Quickloader gave each man 77 rounds of .52 caliber. Every seven shots he had to stop to push in one of the 7 round tubes that fitted through a hole in the stock.

Each trooper also had a Colt army revolver with thirty rounds. Four pack mules carried the company's medical gear such as it was, and another 4,000 rounds for the carbines.

Major Forsyth ate his rations and hoped that the next day would be the time they overtook the Indians.

Meanwhile, about twelve miles upstream on the Arikara, a half dozen Sioux warriors rode into a large encampment of Sioux. There were also a few Cheyenne and Arapahos in the village. The back trail scouts had spotted the soldiers!

The warriors readied their fighting ponies, put on their war paint, called up all the magic they possessed, and put on their clothes and feathers for war.

One of the warriors in the group was a great chief called Bat. He was a head taller than most of the other warriors. He stood six-feet, three-inches, and was heavily muscled and well proportioned. He was the popular leader of the joint band and he claimed his medicine was so strong that no Pony Soldier bullet could harm him.

He led the warriors downstream, after sending out scouts to find the exact location of the Pony Soldier camp.

By morning seven hundred warriors had gathered on the small ridges and bluffs near the Blue Coats' camp. They had the height advantage.

For most attacking forces it would have been an easy fight with a 12 to one advantage. But the Plains Indians lack of military discipline often changed the odds. Too often each man did exactly what he wanted to do, or a small group would decide a battle by doing the wrong or right thing without talking with the war chief.

In this case a small band of Sioux saw a chance to capture the army horses. Horses were the lifeblood of the Sioux nation. A man's wealth was measured by how many horses he had. Whoever captured the horses owned them!

The small group made a surprise attack trying to cut off the horses. The army pickets on guard saw them coming and managed to repulse the attack. The war cries and the firing of the carbines alerted the rest of the Pony Soldiers camp, and the troopers quickly saddled their horses.

Now the Indians swarmed down from the ridges, the enemy seemed to be everywhere. Forsyth calmly surveyed the scene and noticed that the ravine they had ridden through the night before had not been closed by the attacking warriors.

Forsyth had been blooded in Indian fighting methods before and he sensed a trap down the ravine. From the other direction he saw the first mounted attack, a dozen shouting, firing warriors stormed down the dry river bed. It was a ploy to drive them into the ravine. Again the firepower of the repeating Spencers drove the small attacking force off.

"To the island!" Forsyth bellowed. His sergeants heard the command and repeated it, charging the men across the hock deep water of the shallow stream to the sixty-yard long island.

"Form your mounts in a circle and tie them to the brush!" Major Forsyth ordered.

The men quickly saw the reason. Their mounts were forming a living barricade of horseflesh between them and their attackers.

One of the younger troopers panicked. "If we stay here we'll be shot down like dogs!" he screamed.

Forsyth drew his revolver and aimed it at the private. "I'll kill any man who tries to leave!" he bellowed. "This is our only place to make a stand. Look sharp now. When they attack, our job is to kill Indians and their ponies."

Forsyth ordered the men to dig pits behind the horses. They used their hunting knives, tin plates and their hands in the sandy and rocky soil but few got more than a few inches down.

Three sharpshooters had been sent crawling through brush to the upstream point of the island. They lastly worked through tall grass and found open fields of fire upstream from where the first charge by the hostiles would come.

By that time the three troopers on the point could see the red men gathering just out of effective carbine range. Half of the hostiles had rifles, the rest had bows and arrows and lances.

Forsyth figured the Sioux would try to charge the point of the island and simply overrun it, shooting up and cutting down the troopers at close range.

Major Forsyth moved calmly among his men. He remained standing and although occasional shots came from the Indians, no man had yet been wounded.

"Won't be long now, men," he told them. "They'll come hard and fast, so have those Spencers ready. Make every shot count. You have seventy-seven before you reload the tubes. Concentrate on those horses and men heading for the very point of our island."

Then the men called to Forsyth to keep down for his own safety. He found a spot and settled in and waited for the attack.

It came quickly.

A wall of horsemen charged down the shallow sheet of water, splashing great gouts of moisture every which way. The point men and those on each side near that front of the island fired round after round into the charging horsemen.

The attackers took casualties. A horse went down shot through the head and when it fell, three other horses stumbled over it spilling the warriors into the water.

Still they came.

The men poured out a virtual sheet of hot .52 caliber lead at the attacking hostiles. Again and again the men reloaded with the seven shot tubes, and went on firing.

When the front line of red men came almost to the end of the point of land, the fire was so heavy from the Spencer rifles that the wall of riders split and part went down each side of the island.

They had broken the attack!

"Good work, men!" Forsyth called out. "Reload those empty tubes while we have time. This could be a long fight."

Sergeant H. H. McCall crawled over to his commander. "Sir, you're hit in the thigh. Let me tie it up for you."

Forsyth allowed it. Sergeant McCall carried a command presence all his own. During the Civil War he had been a Brevet Brigadier General with a whole Pennsylvania Regiment under his command. In the trim down of the army he had been reduced to his permanent rank of First Sergeant.

Six troopers had been wounded in the first attack. The Indians rode around the island firing again, then moved upstream to ready a new attack.

"Here they come!" one of the lead sharpshooters screeched. Wave after wave of Indian warriors charged the point of land in the middle of the shallow water. Sprays turned the water into a maze of foam and mist.

Again the repeating rifles broke the charge, this time farther way than the first time.

The men cheered, bound up new wounds and reloaded. There were two troopers sprawled in death over and behind the wall of horses. Now all but three of the horses and mules were dead as well.

The tall warrior who commanded the hostiles as head war chief, had not led his men. The man the whites knew as Roman Nose had sat on his horse well away from the fighting and watched.

His horse milled around nervously waiting to do battle. There were hundreds of warriors waiting with him as reserves.

Roman Nose had not led the charge because he told others that his medicine was not right. His magic was not powerful today. He was convinced that if he attacked the troopers that he would die.

Roman Nose knew that usually he was invulnerable to the white eye's bullets. Many times he had ridden through withering fire and not been touched. He had built up a following who knew that he had great medicine, a great magic that turned away both bullet and arrow.

Roman Nose wore into battle a sacred war bonnet that he said gave him his magical invulnerability. There were many sacred taboos and rituals that had to be carried out to maintain the bonnet's power.

When Forsyth's men were approaching the Arikara, Roman Nose had accidentally violated one of the strongest taboos. Now there was no time to engage in the long ritual of purification that would bring back the war bonnet's sacred power.

Roman Nose was afraid to fight that day.

Twice he had seen his brothers fail against the power of the rifles that shoot many times. He was sad, he was angry. Then a great warrior who had charged the island both times and been wounded rode up to Roman Nose and made a sign of disrespect.

"Roman Nose, you are a coward. Your people, your brothers die against the white eyes, and you do nothing!"

It was an insult that had to be answered. Roman Nose kicked his pony into motion, rode down the hill to the river and lifted his heavy rifle over his head with one hand and gave a long war cry.

The Sioux and Cheyenne heard the cry and surged toward their favorite chief. This time he would lead them in the charge. This time with their invincible chief out front they could not fail!

"We will attack, we will win!" Roman Nose shouted.

With those few words and his presence on his large chestnut war pony, he unified the Indians in a way that seldom occurred in the Plains tribes. They shouted and cheered and fell in behind and beside him as another two hundred warriors rushed down the hill to the shallow river. With Roman Nose leading them, they rode in a boiling, shouting, screaming mass toward the three Pony Soldier sharpshooters who still lay unscratched in the weeds at the very point of the little island.

Forsyth had briefed his men. This time they would fire in volleys. He had divided the men into numbers, one's and two's. One group would fire, then the other, then the first. They would continue alternating until they broke the attack or were overrun.

Forsyth looked up and saw the tall man in the saddle and guessed who the war chief was.

"Here they come, men. Make every round count!"

XVI

COLT HAD THE idea as soon as he got up that morning. He wrote it out and mandated that it should be read at a company and troop meeting to all troops before noon. The idea was simple:

"To the men of Ft. Wallace. For some months an illegal and vicious organization called the Brotherhood has been causing trouble, injury and deaths on this post. This is a plea to any man, enlisted or officer, who knows anything about this group to come forward and help us destroy the Brotherhood.

"It will be a double blind, so no one can tell who you are, and no recriminations can be made against you. If you have any information about the deaths of Lieutenant Wilson, Lieutenant Winfield, or Corporal Dennis, please come forward!

"How? There is an unused barracks across from B Infantry Company. In the barracks there are two sergeants' rooms. Go to the first sergeant's room, the one with the door open. In it will be a table and a chair.

"There you will be asked what you wish to tell, and tell it. No one will be in the room. Communications will be through a thick blanket covering a doorway between the rooms. The window will be covered and the room you are in will be dark.

"Come after dark so no one will be able to identify you. We appreciate your help.

"Signed, Colt Harding, Lieutenant Colonel, US Army."

They might get some useful information. The whole purpose of the plan was to trap one or more of the members of the Brotherhood in an attempt on Colt's life. It was tailormade to suit the attackers. They would have darkness outside and in the room. They would have Colt in the next room. One man could burst through the door and gun down anyone waiting and be gone before any alarm could be sounded.

Colt worked most of the morning getting the room ready. Everything he needed was in the barracks. He moved all items except the table and chair from the sergeant's office. Then he tacked an army blanket over the connecting door and the one outside window. In the second sergeant's room, he nailed a blanket over the window. Then brought in four mattresses. These he pushed against the near corner of the room just down from the draped door.

He had not gone with the Lightning Troop that morning on their usual training. He'd needed the time to get his trap ready. Then he went and talked with Colonel Roberts.

The Colonel had not yet fully recovered from the depression his son's suicide had dropped him into, but he brightened at the plan that Colt told him. They agreed on all points.

When the Lightning Troops came back from their training, Colt had a long talk with Lieutenant Phillips. Then the plans were complete.

As soon as it was dark, Colt used a hammer and wrecking bar and as quietly as possible removed the window, frame and all, from the second sergeant's room in the empty barracks. Then he put the blanket back over it.

He had food for the second time that day at the mess. Somehow he had missed out on the noon meal. Back at the empty barracks he went in the side door and left it open. Then he went into the room with the mattresses and sat in a chair against the wall behind the shield of mattresses and waited.

Two hours after dark, he heard someone come in the door. It squeaked, and he hadn't oiled it. He heard a person sit down on the chair.

"You have information?" Colt asked in his normal voice.

"Yes, suh. I know the officers who beat up them two black soldiers."

"Who?"

"Lieutenant Bartlett, he was there and Lieutenant Zennican, and Lieutenant Adams. They done it."

"If those men are arrested and court martialed, will you testify?"

"Oh, no suh. Can't do that. Get kilt."

"I understand. Thanks. Go out the far end of the barracks. Thank you."

The chair scraped, someone walked out and down the barracks. Colt sat back down in the chair and waited again.

An hour later he still waited. Once he nearly went to sleep. He pulled his revolver out and checked it. There were six loads in the cylinder. Tonight he might need all six.

Later, Colt struck a match and checked his pocket watch. It was just after ten o'clock. He had been there four hours. They might not be taking the bait. He'd stay in place until at least one A.M.

His head nodded and he pulled it up, alert. Had he heard something? Yes, footsteps in the barracks. They came closer. Heavy steps, a large man. The chair scraped.

"Anyone here?" a voice asked. It was disguised in some way.

"Sit down and say whatever you want to. No one will know you're here."

"Good." The chair scraped. "I don't know a lot." There was a pause. Colt heard something, a scratch. Then he remembered the sound as he had scratched his match when he looked at his watch. Just beyond the blanket in the other room, a match! A dynamite bomb! He moved silently to the window, stepped through it and jumped to the ground.

He made the call of a night hawk, and heard one come in response. Ahead in the darkness he saw three shadows move closer to the empty barracks.

A six inch fuse would take thirty seconds to burn down. A three inch fuse would be dangerous, but if it burned normally would smoke down in 15 seconds.

A sudden blast shot flames and smoke out the open window of the sergeant's room.

Colt ducked reflexively. When the shards of glass stopped falling, he surged toward the shattered window of the second sergeant's room. It sagged outward. He heard someone smashing at the window frame from inside. A foot kicked out half the remaining frame and a body jumped through. Colt hit the man waist high with a flying tackle and the two went down hard on the ground.

They rolled once, then Colt's .44 pistol muzzle pushed hard into the other man's throat.

"Ease off or you're a dead man where you lay!" Colt bellowed at him. The man relaxed. "Over here," Colt called. "Bring some rope." When Colt had the man tied, he struck a match. "Well, good evening, Lieutenant Zennican. Nice night for a murder, isn't it?"

At the back door of the barracks, Colt found where Lieutenant Phillips and two sergeants had wrestled the man to the ground who ran out that door. When he was tied, Colt struck another match.

"Lieutenant Adams, is his name," Phillips said. "Son of a bitch tried to blow you to pieces!"

At the other door three black troopers held Captain Laughton flat on the ground.

"You ain't going nowheres, Captain suh," one of the Buffalo Soldiers said.

They marched the three to the Officer of the Guard who had come in response to the explosion.

"We need a good strong building where we can keep these three killers locked up," Colt said. "What's your suggestion?"

A half hour later, Colonel Roberts and Colt were ready to question Lieutenant Adams. He had seemed like the best one to start with.

They were in the old powder magazine. It had been built halfway below ground, made of two-by-fours laid sideways above the concrete foundation walls, and had a tongue and groove two-inch ceiling. There were four small rooms for various types of explosives and ammunition.

The rest of the post dynamite and ammunition had been moved into the end room, and a table and two chairs brought in along with four kerosene lamps.

Adams sat at the table, his hands in metal restraints, a look of anger and frustration on his face.

"It wasn't supposed to turn out this way," he said.

"Murder never is, Adams. That was me

you were trying to kill in there tonight. You threw the bomb in the room, right?"

He looked at them without saying a word.

"I figure we hang all three killings on you in one nice neat package. Get it over with. Hell, I don't care if the real killers go free as long as I get one to pay the price."

Adams looked at him with surprise. "What the hell you talking about? I never even joined the group until a week or two ago. I couldn't have done them first two."

"Who cares?" Colt said. "I get the killings blamed on you, Colonel Roberts gets off the hook and so do I, and it's nice and quick and I get back to see my wife and family."

Adams stared at them. "You'd do that? Let the killers go? All I did was help try to blow you up. I didn't even throw the bomb, Zennican did that. And I didn't kill nobody."

"Then who did?" Colt said. "You tell us or you get to look at those seven carbines all aimed at your heart. You won't look long, of course."

"Zennican. I think it was Zennican. He was always bragging about how good he was with that long knife. He claimed that he shut up Winfield. That's the best I can do."

"What about the corporal, the one who took a shot at me and died in the paymaster's old office?"

"Oh, yeah, him. Zennican on that one, I'm certain. I saw him go in, and come out with a big grin on his face."

"But you never actually saw him kill Corporal Dennis?"

"No, but he was alive when Zennican went into the room, and he was dead and on the floor when he came out. I saw that. No, he was on the bunk in there, blood all over the place."

They kept at it for an hour. When they were done, Colt had a whole pad full of notes and statements. He had Adams sign it, then they brought in Captain Laughton.

They used almost the same technique on him. The gist of it was that Laughton accused Adams of all three killings. When Colt pointed out that Adams wasn't even in the group during the first two, he said that Zennican had done all three. Then he changed his story and said that actually Lieutenant Bartlett had been the killer.

They gave up on him. He grinned as he went out. The last man in was Zennican. He refused to talk at all.

With the three men securely locked in

separate rooms in the most secure building at the fort, Colt went to see Lieutenant Bartlett in his quarters.

"Captain Laughton accused you of killing Lieutenant Wilson with the polo mallet."

"Sounds like Laughton. He's been getting crazier as the weeks went by. Laughton killed him. I'll swear to that. I can give you six witnesses who know the same thing. Everyone in that execution polo game. Wilson was a damn nigger lover. He hated all of us and we hated him.

"The polo game was just an excuse. Hell, we'd never played polo before. Made our own mallets and everything. The first time we had a spill it was Wilson who was deliberately knocked down. Laughton went down beside him, whacked him twice with the mallet on his head and it was all over."

"You won't mind writing that down for me and swearing to it?"

"Of course not, but you've got to give me protection."

"That we'll do. Right now we have some more questions, over at the Colonel's office. We want you to write down the names of everyone in the Brotherhood. What they have done, all of it. You might be writing the rest of the night. You do all this and swear to it in the court martial and you won't be charged. You will be transferred to another post, and a reprimand will go in your personnel file."

"Fine, I never killed anybody."

"Let's get over there so we can take care of this. It could be a long night for both of us."

It was. They didn't get finished with Bartlett until almost four A.M. They had all they needed and more for a quick conviction of the two murderers and charges on the others would be pending. They had committed crimes by knowing about the murders and not reporting them.

Colt fell on his bed at last. This could be finished up in a week. He'd give his deposition on the first day of the court martial and be riding out for Fort Leavenworth and home!

An hour later someone banged on his door. It was the corporal of the guard.

"Sir, the Colonel wants you in his office right away. Two scouts on foot have just come in from Major Forsyth's troop. They're in bad trouble and need help!"

XVII

ON THE SMALL island in the middle of the shallow Arikara River in western Colorado, the huge Indian chief called Roman Nose led his hundreds of warriors straight at the 48 cavalrymen under the command of Major George Forsyth. Two of his original men had become ill and had to remain at Ft. Wallace.

"Here they come!" Forsyth called. "Don't fire until you hear my command. Make each shot kill a Sioux! We'll fire by volleys the way we did last time. Good luck."

He waited until the horde of galloping Sioux and Cheyenne were only fifty yards away. They splashed straight for the island in a spraying wall of horses and men.

At fifty yards, Forsyth beat down the pain from his serious thigh bullet wound and bellowed: "Now!"

Hot, angry lead gushed out from the 46 Spencer carbines, slashing into war ponies and Indian attackers at the impossible to miss range. The bullets blasted down horses and riders.

But they came on, wave after wave of them.

The disciplined volley fire meant there was a continual stammering of carbine fire coming from the shallow pits and from behind the troopers' dead horses.

Indian mounts fell now in the front rows, but those riding hard behind them jumped over the dead and dying and surged forward.

The fifth double volley from the cavalrymen staggered the charge and the hostiles wavered and hesitated.

The great chief Roman Nose turned on his big chestnut horse, waved the eight pound rifle over his head in his massive hand, and rallied the Sioux and Cheyenne. They surged forward again.

After the sixth volley from the men on the island, Roman Nose had not been scratched. Then he and a few of his advanced men charged over the point of the island where the three sharpshooters lay hidden.

One of the cavalrymen on the point turned as Roman Nose went past and fired at nearly point blank range. The heavy .52 caliber round caught Roman Nose in the back.

The very force of the heavy ball knocked Roman Nose down. By then a dozen more bullets slammed into his big horse leaving him thrashing in a death struggle in the six-inch deep water near the point of land.

"Hie . . . hie . . . hie . . . hie!" The warriors shouted when they saw their indestructible chief slam into the water and not rise. Roman Nose, the man they knew as Bat, was down, wounded, killed!

Word slashed through the warriors and at once the wave of attackers faltered and fell back, then they parted and swept past the island again.

They had broken the attack again!

Now the mounted Sioux and Cheyenne pulled off to the side out of the effective carbine range and watched the small island. They could see their war chief lying dead in the water. His great chestnut had kicked his way to death in the red stained water beside the chief.

The Indians milled around. It was plain now that there was no one to lead them in another charge. How had the Pony Soldiers all got the long guns that fired-many-times? They shot as fast as the small revolvers.

Back on the island, Major Forsyth looked over his battered band of Pony Soldiers. He had suffered a glancing shot on the head, he had a shattered left shin and couldn't walk. The terrible bullet wound to his right thigh was more serious than he had thought. It hurt him terribly.

He turned to his chief scout. "Can the Sioux do any better than that?" he asked.

"No, sir. In ten years of fighting Indians out here, I've never seen a charge like that one. They can't do any better. Without Roman Nose they'll never even try it again. Now all we have to do is survive."

Lieutenant Frederick Beecher, Forsyth's second in command, dragged himself by his elbows another six feet toward his leader.

"I have suffered my death wound, general!" the young man said softly. Then he looked at the man he had served so well. "Good night," he whispered and died.

The surgeon, Dr. John H. Mooers, who Forsyth had insisted come along to treat his men, was also dying. He had suffered a severe bullet wound to his forehead.

Forsyth tried to get a casualty count. He knew that two of the scouts, Wilson and Culver had been killed and that three more men were dead. That would make at least five dead. He had no idea how many wounded. He could not move around as he wanted to with his shattered foot.

A group of about twenty young warriors split away from the band on the hill and rode hard charging the island from the side, splashing into the narrow ribbon of water at the last moment. But the firing from the troopers cut down four of them and two horses and they turned upstream and rode away.

"Should about do it, sir," the scout said. "They'll keep bothering us, but I don't expect any more full scale charges. They suffered more than they want to already."

Two hours later, Forsyth decided the scout was right. Now and then a small group would try a charge, but be beaten back.

Rifle shots came from the high ground from hidden gunmen. There was no target and the fire kept the troopers hunkered down behind any protection they could find.

From time to time a shower of heavily tipped arrows dropped into the island from warriors who rode up, fired several arrows and retreated. Three men were wounded by the arrows. Forsyth was more worried about the riflemen on the ridges.

There were two more serious charges later

in the day. Indians seemed to come from every side, but each time they were beaten back. There was no Roman Nose to inspire them and lead the charges. When at last the mounted men withdrew, the dismounted Indians along both sides of the ridges continued to send rifle fire into the island.

The men dug their pits deeper into the sand for protection.

At last darkness came and the men had relief from their attackers. These Indians did not believe in fighting at night. They thought if they died at night their souls would wander forever in the darkness.

Now Forsyth checked his situation. He was too good a soldier to leave a position that he had defended so well. If they tried to retreat back toward Ft. Wallace, without any horses, they would be quickly ridden down and slaughtered the next day.

He called for volunteers to walk to Ft. Wallace to bring back a relief troop. Every able bodied man asked to go. Forsyth chose Trudeau, a veteran hunter and plainsman; and Jim Stillwell, a nineteen year old who had fought bravely and given good promise as a scout.

The two men had a hundred and ten mile walk to Ft. Wallace without horses or rations. First they had to get through the Indians who still surrounded them. They both slipped off their boots and tied them around their necks. Then they walked backwards away from the island.

They hoped that if Indians found their footprints in the dust the next day they would assume they were moccasin prints heading for the island.

Once away from the island they crawled on their hands and knees down the banks of the river and to the ravine they had ridden through the day before.

There were still a great many Indians in the area all around the river. They were prepared to fight, but apparently didn't think the trapped force would try to send out any scouts or runners since they would be on foot.

When daylight came, Trudeau and Stillwell had made it only two miles from the island. Indians were all around them. They found a hiding place in a small wash that was within sight of the Indian camps. It was the best they could do.

After almost being discovered twice, the men made it through to darkness, when they began crawling and walking cautiously. It was three days before they felt safe enough to travel without worrying about being captured. Still they hid by day and walked south and east during darkness. Trudeau broke down on the fourth night and Stillwell had to help him as they struggled into Fort Wallace near dawn.

Activity surged. Colonel Roberts assembled a relief force at once. The day before, Colonel Louis H. Carpenter had been sent with seventy men from the Tenth Cavalry H Troop (Negro Troopers) with Lieutenants Banzhaf and Orleman and Doctor Fitzgerald along with 17 scouts and thirteen wagons and an ambulance to move out along the Denver trail some 60 miles and set up a camp. They would protect the Denver wagon trail, hold off Indians, scout in all directions for hostiles, and give assistance to travelers on the way to Denver.

A messenger was sent to Colonel Carpenter to proceed at once to the third tributary of the Republican and to give relief to Major Forsyth. He had everything that he needed and could make quick time. Another relief column headed out from Ft. Wallace but would not be able to get to the trapped men as quickly as Carpenter.

Colt was instructed to take the Lightning Troop and proceed quickly to the same area to offer support. It was 110 miles away. He would take the scout Stillwell with him to show him the quickest way to the trapped men.

"Forsyth and his men have been pinned down there for five days now," Colt told the men.

They had been routed out of bed at five A.M. to get ready for the ride. Now, scarcely an hour later, they were outfitted, saddled and sitting in formation in front of a somber Colonel Colt Harding.

"We'll do fifty-five miles a day for two days and be there. You've wanted some action, this will be a chance to prove yourselves."

The men cheered. They had been recruited after the war to go to the West and fight Indians. It was the 10th's first time on a real battle patrol, but would be far from the last. They were fit, trained and ready.

They gained a high point overlooking a long slice of country early in the third day out from the fort. Far ahead, Colt could see a valley and a narrow bright silver streak of river coursing through the middle.

In the center of the stream lay a small island. Stillwell, who had just walked for four days to give the alarm about Major

Forsyth, had returned to guide them. He recognized the small island with the cottonwood on the end.

"That's it! Christ, let's hurry!" he bellowed.

Colt led his troop down toward the stream and then up to the island. They could see men moving about and others slumped on the ground.

Stillwell charged across the river into the pits to the cheers of the men.

Colt's men quickly followed and they emptied their saddlebags giving the men the special rations they had brought along for them. They ate anything they could get their hands on, hardtack, bacon and salt pork. An hour later the rescue team from Colonel Carpenter of thirty troops came over the rise with one ambulance loaded with hardtack, coffee and bacon.

Colt ordered his Pony Soldiers mounted and they rode up to the ridges on both sides to be sure that the Indians had really pulled out. They swept the ridges for three miles, returning with the word that only bits and pieces of pottery and a few tipi stakes were found indicating the Indians had left in a hurry sometime ago.

As the men ate, another army column

came over the hill. The rest of the thirteen wagons with Colonel Carpenter's column had arrived with the surgeon and his supplies. He quickly went about patching up those he could save and setting the several that were beyond help at peace.

Some of the men told about Major Forsyth:

"His leg got worse and worse where he took the rifle round. It was in deep, pressing against an artery. He ordered several of us to cut it out, but nobody would. It was so deep we feared we would cut the artery and kill him.

"On the fourth day he asked for his saddlebags and took out his razor. He ordered two men to hold the wound apart and with his razor carved into his own flesh until he worked out the bullet. He had nothing to deaden the pain, not even a bottle of whiskey."

Survivors said that the Indians had kept up the attack for four days, and after that they could see the Indian women and children pulling out of the area. It was a good sign. The warriors had decided the price was too high for a victory, and would soon leave. The last four or five days the Forsyth men were not attacked by Indians, but they had to try to survive. Food was their biggest need.

The horseflesh they had been eating to stay alive, now became putrid and the smell was terrible. One coyote had wandered close and was shot and eaten, but no more game came near them. At least there was plenty of water to drink. This alone was one factor that saved their lives.

The men who were fit to travel were told by Major Forsyth they could leave and work their way to Fort Wallace, but they had refused, and even though they were not a regular cavalry troop, they had developed a strong loyalty to the officer and the other men and swore to stay by his side until help arrived or until they all died.

Major Forsyth's troop had been authorized by General Sheridan for special duty. No organized troop leader would surrender command of his troop to the major, so he was told to recruit his own from frontiersman, former soldiers and scouts. He did, picking and choosing from a host of volunteers. He picked 20 at Ft. Hayes and thirty more at Ft. Harker. He was assigned Lieutenant Beecher as his Second in Command, his First Sergeant, the surgeon, and the guide for the group was Sharp Grover.

Half of those picked for the troop had been former officers in the Civil War, and the rest were hunters and trappers. They were not held to strict military discipline, but knew how to fight well.

By the time they were rescued many of the men were in sorely bad condition. Major Forsyth had developed a high fever. Only the doctor being along on the rescue column saved his and several other of the men's lives.

The trip back to Ft. Wallace on the wagons proved to be almost as hard and painful a ride as the fight itself. They jolted and bounced in the wagons, but they were safe and going back to the fort. It took four long days to make the trip over the raw and unbroken country where there were no roads.

Colt and the Buffalo Soldiers operated as escort for the procession. While they met no opposition on the rescue mission, Colt was proud of his Lightning Troop. He was sure they would give a good account for themselves in their first action against the hostiles.

XVIII

FOR THREE DAYS after the relief parties rode into Ft. Wallace, the post was buzzing with talk of the fight and the terrible price the Cheyenne and Sioux had paid. The stories about the battle grew with each telling. Major Forsyth made his official report and had it sent by telegraph directly to General Sheridan at Ft. Hayes, Kansas.

The telegraph line had been extended down to the fort from the end of the Kansas Pacific Railroad tracks and had been almost constantly busy since the troops returned. News of the great victory for the Pony Soldiers flashed across the nation, hit the newspapers, and was the gist of talk around every army post in the west. They called it the battle of Beecher's Island, after Lieutenant Beecher who died there.

At last the Pony Soldiers had an epic battle to talk about, one that they had won, and one that cost the Indians at least two hundred dead, as the scouts on the mission had calculated.

The more he heard about the battle from the various men who had fought there, the more certain Colt was that it would go down in history as one of the important engagements of the Indian Wars. Not because the stand had won land or saved an important fort, but because a small band of Pony Soldiers with superior weapons had dug into a well defended position, and stood off over 700 hostiles. It was the first time in the history of the Indian Wars that the United States Army troops had a great victory to shout about.

Colt looked at his kitchen table and found stacks of material. He had ignored it for two days as he rested, took a bath, and tried to get back on schedule.

Now he carefully checked the stacks of court martial material that was being prepared. Much of it was awaiting his signature. He settled down to the task. It was still his hope that he could give his testimony and have it written down for later presentation to the court martial. He had done this in various cases before.

He looked at the crimes.

Captain Laughton would be charged with

the murder of Lieutenant Wilson. Lieutenant Zennican would be charged with the killing of Lieutenant Winfield and the bushwhacker, Corporal Dennis. That much was easy, clear and certain.

But how should the other officers in the Brotherhood be charged? Conspiracy, for sure. All of them had participated in a murder conspiracy to seize and kill the three men.

As a less serious charge they all could be found guilty of having knowledge of the three murders and the beating, even if they did not participate in any of them. Colt pondered it for the rest of the day and then went to talk to Colonel Roberts in his quarters.

"Hell, we should rack their asses!" Roberts barked. "The fuckers pissed all over the Officer Corps by doing this. Makes us all look bad."

Colt nodded and sipped at the drink. "True, but if we charge eight more officers, what's that going to do to the spirit and the morale of the officers and men around here?"

"Jesus, shoot it to hell!"

"About the size of it. Maybe we can come down hard on the two, and put reprimands in the permanent files of the others. Would that serve justice?"

"Hell, no!" Colonel Roberts blustered. "I want the bastards who beat up that Negro, too. But I know I can't have it all. I do want a complete confession from every man in that Brotherhood to hold onto as long as I need to. None of them is going to get a promotion on this post. And I won't let them transfer. I'll ride them for years!"

"Now we're talking army justice," Colt said with a grin. "I'll get back to that court martial paperwork and get it all ready for your orderly to make copies of. Then I think it'd be a good idea for you to send a telegram to General Sheridan letting him know that the situation here is rapidly clearing up."

"Sounds reasonable." Colonel Roberts shook his head. "Damn, but that must have been something to see! Those forty-eight Spencer carbines slamming out lead at that Indian charge. Did you say seven-damn-hundred hostiles against the forty-eight troopers?"

"True, but only on the first charge. They lost some men that first charge and the men who couldn't fire gave their Spencers to those who could. Less shooters after that. Forsyth sure held those irregulars together. He even told the healthy ones to strike out for the fort once the hostiles had left. They said they wouldn't go without the wounded, which they all knew was impossible."

"Damn fine bunch of men. Wonder what Phil Sheridan will do with them now? It's going to take a long time for Forsyth to heal up and be ready for duty."

"Doc Judson told him not to count on doing much of anything for a year, maybe two."

Colt rubbed his jaw. He didn't know whether to tell Roberts about one of the things that Lieutenant Bartlett had told him or not during that long night of confession. At last he decided to go ahead.

"In Bartlett's confession he said that your son had talked to him about joining the Brotherhood. He said he figured it was a little strange since Lieutenant Roberts hadn't shown much sign of being a Negro hater before.

"They talked a few times and Bartlett invited Leroy to come to a session. It was the one when they beat up on the Negro boy who had smashed up the white kid.

"Bartlett said after Leroy saw the first couple of blows struck against the tied up Negro man, he said, 'This isn't for me,' and left. Bartlett said he told Leroy to be sure not to mention a word about it. Leroy swore that he never would. I thought you should know about this."

Colonel Roberts had turned away when the talk began about Leroy. Now he swung around and wiped his eyes. "I'm glad to know. I gave my son an assignment to try to get into the Brotherhood. He was doing it even though he hated the whole idea. I pushed him, I guess I pushed him too hard. I always tried to make him into something that he wasn't."

"Lots of us do that with our children," Colt said. "He was more of a man than any of us. He walked away from the group and knew they would be watching him. You can be proud of him, sir."

"Do you think that not being able to join that group had anything to do with his . . . his taking his own life?"

"No, sir. Not a chance. It couldn't have had a thing to do with a decision like that."

The next morning, Colt went to the telegrapher's room and sent a wire to General

Sheridan where he had moved up to Fort Hays.

SITUATION HERE RESOLVED STOP REQUEST A TWO MONTH'S LEAVE WITH MY FAMILY AT FORT LEAVENWORTH STOP COLONEL ROBERTS TAKING CONTROL OF THE SITUATION HERE STOP TWO OFFICERS CHARGED WITH MURDER AND COURT MARTIALS BEING PREPARED STOP ASK TO BE RELIEVED OF MY DUTY HERE AT EARLIEST OPPORTUNITY STOP SIGNED LIEUTENANT COLONEL COLT HARDING STOP SPECIAL ASSIGNMENT END

Colt went back to his quarters and finished writing up the charges against the two officers, and then worked out a sample of the reprimand that would go in the permanent file of every officer who participated in the Brotherhood.

He went back to the Fort Commander's office.

"One thing I forgot to tell you last night. I made a deal with Lieutenant Bartlett that if he confessed to everything and testified against the members of the Brotherhood, he would receive immunity from any court martial. With that in mind, I suggest that

Lieutenant Bartlett be transferred to another post. The men will soon know he was the one who talked and named them. He will have to testify in the court martial. It will be impossible to insure his safety on this post."

Colonel Roberts was drawing a picture on a pad of paper. He was rather good with a pencil. He looked up and nodded. "Yeah, I'm sure he would get his head beaten in a few times. Might do it myself. Never have liked that little bastard myself. I'll put him on the wire and see where I can send him just as soon as the court martials are over."

He looked up and grinned. "Heard you sent a wire to General Phil this morning. Your job is done here so you're pulling out I'd say, right?"

"About right. This should take care of any chance that you'll be losing the post. Now all you have to do is try to keep the officers happy who are working with the Buffalo Soldiers. Those Negro troopers are sharp, good fighters. Before long you'll have officers standing in line to lead the Negro troops."

"Might at that. How's the Lightning Troop?"

"Damn good, and getting better every day. By the time they finish the training and go out chasing hostiles, they'll be some of the best fighters in the army. Be sure they keep doing their target practice.

"Wouldn't hurt the rest of your units to do some as well. Helps when a trooper or a soldier can hit what he aims at." Colt grinned and left to talk to the Lightning troops.

That evening he wrote a long letter to Doris, telling her that he hoped he would be on the train heading home soon. He thought of the past year. It had been a pivotal one in his career. From the days at Ft. Comfort in Western Texas, those terrible days when he had lost his first wife and his son and his only daughter, Sadie, had been captured and taken into the mountains by the Comanche.

At last he had rescued her, and at the same time rescued a woman who soon became his wife. The small orphan boy they brought with them became their adopted son to complete their family.

Colt thought about his small family. He wanted to see them all, right now!

He began cleaning up his things, packing what he owned in his one large leather traveling case, and putting the gear he had drawn from the fort in another pile. When he had that arranged, he went to the Commander's office and talked to First Sergeant Clarnerlet.

"Just when does the next train leave Wallace?" Colt asked.

"Sir, there's a daily train that leaves at ten-thirty A.M. There usually is no problem finding a seat."

Colt grinned. His orders were rather flexible. He'd drop in on General Phil Sheridan at Ft. Hays sometime tomorrow and ask him in person about that two month leave. The winter offensive he knew Sheridan was planning wouldn't warm up for a couple of months anyway. He would be about ready for it.

Colt told Colonel Roberts he was leaving the next day.

"You given us all the testimony that you need to?" Roberts asked. "Let's check those court martials, and the parts you were in on personally. You give us any depositions we need today, and I won't even grab your sleeve when you get on that train."

The next morning, Lieutenant Colonel Colt Harding settled down in the coach train seat and watched as it pulled out of Wallace,

Kansas. A short stop in Ft. Hays, and the next day he would be home in Ft. Leavenworth. Yeah! About time.

He wasn't even going to think about his next assignment with the Pony Soldiers for General Phil Sheridan!